JONATHAN MERES

THE WORLD OF
NORM

MAY PRODUCE GAS

ORCHARD

To Drew who cannot wait.

CHAPTER 1

Norm knew it was going to be one of those days when he woke up and got blamed for global warming.

"What?" said Norm.

"You heard," said Norm's dad, spraying a mouthful of toast and marmalade across the table.

Norm's dad was right. Norm *had* heard. He just needed to check. "Global warming is **my** fault?" said Norm, who was perfectly used to being blamed for all kinds of stuff – just not stuff quite on this scale.

Norm's dad nodded and took another bite of toast.

"What? All of it?" said Norm.

"That's not what I said, Norman."

Funny, thought Norm. Because as far as he was concerned, that was *exactly* what his dad had said. That Norm – and Norm alone – was single-handedly responsible for the imminent destruction of the *entire* planet.

"All I did was leave the TV on standby, Dad."

"And you left the light on overnight."

Norm shrugged. "It's just a light, Dad. It's no biggie."

"It's *not* just a light, Norman."

Norm pulled a face. "What is it then?"

"It's the tip of the iceberg," said Norm's dad. "No pun intended."

Iceberg? thought Norm. What flipping iceberg? And what flipping pun? What on earth was his dad on about?

"What I'm saying," said Norm's dad, "is that if you carry on like this, there'll **be** no icebergs."

Norm pulled another face. He never had been any good at puzzles. He **hated** puzzles! Puzzles were for geeks. What was the connection between leaving a light on, and icebergs? Frankly, who cared? Norm certainly didn't. Especially first thing on a Saturday morning.

"Do I need to spell it out, Norman?"

"What? **Iceberg?**" said Norm.

"It's a waste of energy," said Norm's dad, spraying another mouthful of toast and marmalade.

It's a waste of flipping food, thought Norm who was beginning to wish he had an umbrella with him. How come his *dad* was allowed to speak with his mouth full, but not **him?**

"Switch things **off** when you're not using them!" said Norm's dad. "**Save** energy – don't **waste** it!"

"Whatever," said Norm.

"No, Norman. Not **whatever**," said Norm's dad. "I presume you've heard of the greenhouse effect?"

Whoa, thought Norm. His dad was seriously beginning to lose the plot now. What was he going on about flipping greenhouses for? They didn't even **have** a greenhouse!

"All the gases building up in the earth's atmosphere?" said Norm's dad.

Norm was beginning to feel gas build up a lot closer to home. If he didn't get to the bathroom soon there was likely to be some very **localised** global warming.

"Temperatures rising?" said Norm's dad.

"Yeah, but that's a good thing, right?" said Norm.

"How exactly is that a good thing, Norman?"

Norm thought for a moment. "Well, if it was warmer there'd be no need to go abroad on holiday. There'd be less planes in the sky. Less pollution."

Norm had no idea whether what he'd just said was right or not. It sounded reasonable enough though.

"That's not the point," said Norm's dad. "The point is, you should switch things off when you're not using them. It saves **money**!"

Aha! thought Norm. So *that's* what this was all about. He might have known. Never mind all that global-warming-save-the-flipping-planet guff. It was all about saving **money!** It always flipping was these days. It was so unfair! Why should Norm have to suffer just because his stupid dad had gone and got himself sacked?

"If you don't start remembering to switch things off, I'm going to..."

Norm's dad stopped mid-sentence.

"I'm going to..."

Norm knew exactly what **he'd** do if he didn't get to the bathroom very soon. And besides, he wasn't particularly bothered *what* his dad said he was going to do. He never carried out any of the threats he made. He might as well threaten to make Norm wear a dress and call him Kylie. He was never actually going to do it.

"I'm going to…"

"What, Dad?" said Norm.

Norm's dad sighed. "I'll think of something. Just remember to switch things off. That's all there is to it!"

"But…"

"No buts, Norman!" said Norm's dad, the vein on the side of his head beginning to throb – a sure-fire sign that he was starting to get stressed. Not that Norm noticed. He knew it was useless arguing, though. He might as well just let his dad say what

he'd got to say and get it over with. The sooner his dad got it over with the sooner Norm could go. And boy did Norm need to go! And anyway, so what if he was being blamed for global warming? It wasn't the end of the world.

Norm chuckled to himself.

"What's so funny?" said Norm's dad.

"It's not the end of the world," said Norm.

"What isn't?"

"Being blamed for global warming."

Norm's dad looked blankly at Norm.

"Geddit?" said Norm.

"It's no laughing matter, Norman. Just switch things off in future, right?"

12

Norm sighed.

"Right?" said Norm's dad.

"Right, Dad."

"And remember to close doors behind you."

"Uh?" said Norm.

"It's what they're for!"

"What **what** are for?"

"Doors," said Norm's dad. "They're not meant to be left open. They're meant to be closed. Otherwise what's the point of having them?"

Norm had literally no idea what his dad was talking about any more. Not that he ever had **much** idea what his dad was talking about. But now it was as if he was watching a foreign movie. **Without** subtitles.

"Doors help keep the heat in," said Norm's dad. "They help to save money! If you're going to leave them open all the time I might as well just set fire to twenty-pound notes!"

That would be one way of keeping warm, thought Norm, getting up and heading for the stairs.

"Where are you going?" said Norm's dad. "I haven't finished."

"Toilet," said Norm without bothering to turn round.

"Only flush if necessary," said Norm's dad.

It was going to be necessary all right, thought Norm. It was going to be abso-flipping-lutely necessary.

"Saves money! I mean, water!" yelled Norm's dad. "And shut the door behind you!"

But it was too late. Norm had already gone.

CHAPTER 2

Norm was sat reading a mountain-biking magazine when there was an urgent knock on the door.

"Is that you in there, Norman?" said a muffled voice.

Norm would have known that voice anywhere – no matter how muffled it was. It was Brian's – and there was something uniquely annoying about Brian's voice. Then again, thought Norm, there was something uniquely annoying about Brian.

Norm turned a page. Whatever his middle brother wanted would just have to wait.

"I know it's you, Norman!" said Brian, beginning to sound more and more agitated.

Norm sighed. Couldn't a guy get a moment's peace without being hassled? Was that really too much to ask? Apparently it was.

There was another knock on the door – this time louder, longer and if anything, even more urgent.

"What are you *doing* in there?"

Enough was enough. Norm's levels of patience had just hit rock bottom.

"What do you flipping *think* I'm doing, you little freak?" yelled Norm. "I'm on the flipping toilet!"

"Language," said another voice – this one closer and distinctly *un*muffled.

Norm looked round to find Dave lying in the bath, his head barely visible above a mini mountain range of bubbles.

This was getting ridiculous, thought Norm. In fact never mind **getting** ridiculous – it had already **got** ridiculous. He was nearly thirteen years old! Surely he was entitled to **some** privacy, wasn't he? In fact, never mind flipping privacy – this was a serious breach of basic human rights.

"What are **you** doing here?"

"What does it look like I'm doing?" said Dave.

"Having a bath," said Norm.

"So why ask then?" said Dave.

Norm sighed. It wasn't *his* fault they'd only got one toilet in this stupid little house –and that it was in the bathroom. In their old house they'd had a **separate** toilet. It had been possible for someone to have a bath *and* someone to have a pee at the same time! Not any flipping more it wasn't! It was like living in the flipping Stone Age or something. Virtually everybody Norm knew had a separate toilet and bathroom. Mikey's parents had their *own* bathroom. His perfect flipping cousins *all* had their own bathrooms! It was *so* unfair!

"I'm going to wet myself in a minute!" shouted Brian.

"Good," muttered Norm.

"You're taking too long!"

Too long? thought Norm. Since when had there been a time limit?

"How much longer are you going to be?"

"As long as it takes," snapped Norm through gritted teeth.

"Well, hurry up," said Brian.

"Else what?" said Norm. "What are you going to do about it, Brian? Give me a ticket?"

"Uh?" said Brian.

"What are you, Brian? Some kind of toilet warden?"

"Seriously, Norman, I'm telling Mum and Dad if you don't let me in," said Brian.

"Seriously, Brian, I don't flipping care!" said Norm, turning another page. "Now shut up. I'm trying to read."

"I thought you were..."

"Are you still here?" said Norm.

"MUM! DAD!" "Norman's taking too long in the toilet!!"

There was a sudden clatter of footsteps up the stairs.

"How much longer are you going to be in there, love?" said Norm's mum.

This was seriously beginning to do Norm's head in. Why was everyone so obsessed with how long he was going to be on the flipping toilet? Didn't they have better things to do? He had no *idea* how long he was going to be on the flipping toilet! A flipping long time at this rate!

"You heard your mother," said Norm's dad. "How much longer are you going to be?"

Gordon flipping Bennet, thought Norm. Who else was out there? Why didn't they invite the flipping neighbours round while they were at it? In fact, why stop there? Why not just invite the whole street round!

"We're going to IKEA, remember?" said Norm's mum.

What? thought Norm. IKEA? On a Saturday morning? When he could be at Mikey's? Never mind the end of the world. This was *worse* than the end of the world. This made the end of the world seem like a picnic in the park by comparison. What did they need to go to IKEA for again, anyway? There was no room left in the house for anything else. It was full to flipping bursting point already.

"Psst! Norman!" hissed Dave.

Norm turned to find his youngest brother pulling a funny face and frantically gesticulating towards the window. Surely the smell wasn't ***that*** bad, was it?

And then Norm suddenly twigged. Dave wasn't about to be overcome by fumes. He was trying to tell him something! The window! The perfect means of escape! The *only* means of escape! It was just a short drop down onto the garage roof. And from the garage roof he could shin down the drainpipe and be away on his bike before anyone knew it. He hadn't actually said anything to his parents yet. They didn't know for sure that he was even in there.

"I'm warning you, Norman!" said Norm's dad, his voice getting higher and higher. "Answer me now! How much longer are you going to be in there?"

"He's not in here!" yelled Dave. "It's *me* in here!"

"What?" said Norm's dad, managing to sound both muffled *and* puzzled at the same time.

"Norman's not in here, Dad! It's me! Dave!"

"Where is he?"

"No idea, Dad!" said Dave.

Norm smiled at Dave. But this was no time to stop and wonder *why* his little brother had done what he'd done. All Norm knew was that he needed to act quickly if he was to get away with it.

Norm stood up. Dave immediately disappeared beneath the bubbles. He had no more desire to see what Norm needed to do, than Norm had to be *seen* doing what he needed to do. By the time Dave resurfaced, Norm had gone.

CHAPTER 3

"Hello, **Norman**," said an all-too-familiar voice from the other side of the fence, as Norm slid down the drainpipe and landed on the ground.

Norm didn't need to bother turning round to know that it was Chelsea. So he didn't bother.

"Sssshhh!" hissed Norm, opening the garage door as quietly as possible.

"All right, all right," said Chelsea. "Keep your hair on, **Norman**."

It never failed to annoy Norm, the way that Chelsea always deliberately overemphasised his name like it was the funniest name she'd ever heard. Thank goodness she only lived next door with her dad at weekends. If she ever moved in permanently, Norm would have to seriously consider emigrating.

"What's with all the Mission Impossible stuff?"

"What?" said Norm, putting his helmet on.

"You know – all the climbing out of the window and sliding down the drainpipe? It's all a bit James Bond, isn't it?"

"I'll tell you what it is," said Norm. "It's none of your flipping business, that's what it is."

"Ooooh!" said Chelsea sarcastically.

Norm pursed his lips but said nothing. Now wasn't the time for any kind of blazing argument with Chelsea. Now was the time to get on his bike and ride – as quickly and with as little fuss as possible. **Before** his parents saw him! But that wasn't easy when your occasional next-door neighbour just happened to be **the** most annoying person in the whole wide flipping world.

"So where's the fire?"

"Uh?" said Norm.
"What are you on about?"

"What's the hurry?"
said Chelsea.

Norm sighed. "Which part
of **none of your business**
do you not understand?"

Chelsea smiled. "I just like to know these things,
that's all, **Norman**. No need to get you pants in
a palaver!"

"What?" said Norm.

"Your knickers in a twist,"
said Chelsea.

Norm sighed again. "If you **must** know, I'm not
going to IKEA."

"What do you mean, you're *not* going to IKEA?"
said Chelsea. "I'm not going to China."

"I mean, everyone **else** is going to IKEA – but I'm not," said Norm.

"Oh, I see," said Chelsea. "So where **are** you going?"

"Mikey's," said Norm, wheeling his bike out of the garage and closing the door as quietly as possible.

"Oh right, Mikey's, eh?" said Chelsea.

Norm got on his bike.

"How is he?"

"I've no idea," said Norm. "I've not got there yet."

"Well, when you do…" began Chelsea.

"**If** I flipping do," muttered Norm.

"…be sure to say hi."

Norm pulled a face. Of course he'd say hi to Mikey. Why **wouldn't** he say hi to Mikey? What kind of stupid thing was that to say?

"From me, I mean," said Chelsea as if she'd been reading Norm's mind.

"I knew that," said Norm.

"So why aren't you going to IKEA?"

"Don't want to."

"Why not?"

Norm shrugged. "Just don't want to."

"Yes, but why not?" persisted Chelsea.

"Because I've got better things to do," said Norm, finding it increasingly difficult to keep his voice down.

"Like, what?"

Norm took a deep breath. One more stupid question and he was going to blow a flipping fuse. But if Chelsea actually asked another question Norm didn't hear it, because at that moment loud throbbing rock music started to blast out of his trousers.

"Hello?" said Norm, answering his phone as quickly as possible, whilst making a mental note to change his ringtone to something quieter. "Oh, hi, Mum."

Chelsea smiled knowingly at Norm.

"Where am I? Erm, at Mikey's, Mum" said Norm. He glared at Chelsea, defying her to say anything.

"Oh, really? IKEA?" said Norm, doing his best to sound disappointed. "Sorry, Mum, I had no idea. I would have loved to have come."

Norm listened for a moment before his jaw suddenly dropped and his eyes opened wide in a look of sheer terror.

"No, no, no, there's no need to come and pick me up, Mum! Honest! I'll be fine!"

Norm listened some more.

"I know it's a shame, Mum. But there's always the next time, eh?"

Norm needed to wrap things up, and fast. If he hung around much longer, his parents would see him and he really **would** be going to IKEA!

"Ooh, gotta go, Mum. Mikey's calling me. Catch you later, Mum. Bye."

Norm ended the call, pocketed his phone again and set off on his bike. He didn't need to bother turning round to know that
Chelsea would be smiling
at him in that oh-so-
annoying way of hers.
So he didn't bother.

CHAPTER 4

"He said **what?**" said Mikey, one eyebrow raised in
surprise like a small, furry caterpillar
doing a press-up.

"That global warming's my
fault," said Norm, matter-
of-factly.

"What? All of it?" said Mikey.

Norm nodded. "Apparently, yeah."

"That's a bit harsh, isn't it?" said Mikey.

"Tell me about it," said Norm.

Mikey and Norm were sat side by side in Mikey's
room. Mikey was playing FIFA on the Xbox. Norm

was on Mikey's laptop, looking at mountain-biking videos on YouTube.

"How come?" said Mikey.

"How come, what?" said Norm.

"Global warming's all your fault?"

"Oh, right," said Norm. "Dunno. Something about leaving lights on and icebergs."

"Uh?" said Mikey, screwing up his face.

"Exactly," said Norm. "He might as well have been talking Belgian."

Mikey turned to Norm like he wasn't quite sure whether to say what he was about to say or not.

"Er..."

"What?" said Norm.

"You *do* know there's no such language as Belgian, don't you, Norm?"

"Uh?" said Norm.

"You know that some Belgians speak French and some speak Flemish."

"Course I knew that," said Norm even though he clearly didn't and even though he actually couldn't care less. "What do you think I am, Mikey? Stupid or something?"

"Sorry," said Mikey. "I knew you knew that."

"Whatever," said Norm, who had a pretty good idea that Mikey knew that he *didn't* know that – but was much too nice to say.

"It's quite interesting though, isn't it?"

"What is?"

"That there's no such actual language as Belgian in Belgium."

Norm turned to his best friend and looked at him like he'd just announced that he'd been a penguin in a previous life.

"You seriously think that's interesting, Mikey?"

"Yeah, course," said Mikey. "Don't you?"

"It's one of the most *boring* things I've ever heard," said Norm.

"Really?" said Mikey.

"Not really," said Norm. "It's **the** most boring thing I've ever heard."

Mikey laughed.

"I'm serious!" said Norm. "Honestly, Mikey, if you think **that's** interesting you need to see a flipping doctor."

Mikey laughed again.

"Mikey?" said Norm.

"What?" said Mikey.

"Shut up!"

Mikey shut up and for the next few minutes they carried on doing what they'd been doing – Mikey playing FIFA and Norm watching biking videos. Eventually, though, Mikey's curiosity got the better of him.

"So?"

"So what?" said Norm.

"What happened?"

"When?"

"When you got blamed for global warming?"

"What do you mean?" said Norm.

"I mean, what's your dad going to do about it?"

Norm shrugged. "Dunno. Nothing probably."

"Nothing?" said Mikey.

"Probably, yeah," said Norm. "I mean, he's always **threatening** to do stuff as a punishment. But he never actually goes ahead and does it. He's all talk."

"Whoa," said Mikey. "My parents **always** carry out their threats."

"Oh, yeah?" said Norm, who couldn't imagine Mikey's mum and dad even **threatening** to do anything – let alone actually going ahead and doing it. Mikey's mum and dad were quite possibly the nicest people in the whole wide world. **They** hadn't had to move to a smaller house because Mikey's dad had been fired. **They** didn't have to buy flipping supermarket own-brand coco pops. Best of all though, as far as Norm was concerned, Mikey's mum and dad had been sensible enough not to have any more kids after Mikey. Mikey was an **only** child. **He** never got into trouble for stuff his annoying little brothers did. Jammy doughnut, thought Norm, who would have given **anything** to be an only child again. Even for a day or so. Just to see what it felt like again.

Did Mikey realise just how flipping lucky he was?

"You'd be surprised how strict my parents can be sometimes," said Mikey.

"Your parents?" laughed Norm. "Strict? Are you serious?"

"Totally," said Mikey. "You only ever see one side of them, Norm. You don't see them after you've gone."

"Obviously," said Norm.

"Mum threw a complete wobbly the other day."

 Mikey nodded.

"I don't believe you, Mikey."

"No, really, she did," said Mikey.

"Why?" said Norm.

Mikey hesitated. "I'd rather not say."

"Why not?"

"It's a bit...you know?"

"No, I don't know actually," said Norm. "That's why I'm flipping asking!"

"It's a bit..."

"A bit *what?*"

"Embarrassing," mumbled Mikey.

Norm grinned.

"Shut up, Norm," said Mikey.

"I didn't say anything," said Norm.

"You were about to," said Mikey.

True, thought Norm. He **had** been about to say something. As soon as he'd thought of something suitably sarcastic. What could Mikey have done that was so embarrassing and caused his mum to throw a so-called "wobbly"?

"Well?" said Norm. "Are you going to tell me, or am I going to have to guess?"

"Guess," mumbled Mikey.

"Guess what?" said Mikey's mum, appearing in the doorway carrying two mugs of hot chocolate.

Norm's eyes widened, all thoughts of Mikey's embarrassment – and everything else for that matter – temporarily banished to the very back of his mind. Norm had one thought and one thought alone. Namely, to get that hot chocolate down his neck as fast as possible. Mikey's mum's hot chocolate was the best ever. It was the stuff of legend. It was to die for. Well, not actually **die** for. But to pay good money for, anyway. If Norm actually **had** any money, of course. Which he didn't.

"Doesn't matter, Mum," said Mikey, clearly trying to avoid the subject.

"Hello, Norman, by the way."

"Hello, Mikey's mum," Norm just about managed to croak.

"I thought you might like a little energy boost. Growing boys like you."

"Thanks, Mum," said Mikey.

Norm didn't say anything. Norm **couldn't** say anything. Any minute now he was going to start drooling. Things could get very messy.

Mikey's mum took a couple of steps into the room, then stopped and sniffed.

Sniff

Sniff

"Phwoar!" she said. "You've been doing it again, haven't you, Mikey?"

Doing what? thought Norm.

"Sorry, Mum," said Mikey, instantly going bright red.

"I've told you before. Stynx is a **deodorant** – not an air freshener."

"Sorry, Mum," said Mikey, by now the colour of an overripe tomato.

"Please try and remember in future."

"I will, Mum," said Mikey. "Sorry."

Mikey's mum smiled sweetly and put the two mugs of hot chocolate down on Mikey's desk.

"I'll leave you to it then, boys," she said, heading for the door again. "See you later."

"Bye, Mum," said Mikey.

Mikey waited for his mum to disappear before turning to Norm.

"See?"

Norm pulled a face. "See what?"

"What do you mean, see what?" said Mikey. "She just went ballistic!"

Norm was gobsmacked. This had to be a wind-up. Any minute now Mikey was going to crack up laughing. Norm waited. And waited. And waited.

"You're joking, right?" said Norm.

"Joking?" said Mikey. "I'm not joking."

Norm shook his head in disbelief. If that was Mikey's idea of ballistic then he was an even bigger and jammier doughnut than he'd previously thought. Norm's mum went more ballistic than that if someone left the flipping toilet seat up.

"You have **no** idea, Mikey."

"You won't tell anyone, will you, Norm?"

"What? You mean, about your mum going 'ballistic'?" said Norm, making speech marks in the air with his fingers. "Don't worry. Your secret's safe with me."

Mikey hesitated as if, once again, he was unsure whether to say what he was about to say or not.

"I mean, about the deodorant."

Norm stared at Mikey for a moment.

"Is *that* what you're embarrassed about?"

Mikey nodded.

"You're embarrassed because you use deodorant?"

Mikey nodded again. "Got to."

"What do you mean, you've *got* to?" said Norm.

"I'm starting to stink."

Norm leaned over and sniffed
Mikey a couple of times.

"No you're not."

"Are you sure?" said Mikey.

"Positive," said Norm.

"You must be blocked up," said Mikey.

Norm sniffed again. "No I'm not. I can smell that hot chocolate! Now, if you'll excuse me..."

Norm picked up a mug and took a sip. As he did so he closed his eyes, all negative thoughts evaporating from him like steam from a kettle. If anything, Mikey's mum's hot chocolate was even more delicious than usual. And that was flipping saying something.

"I think I might be changing," said Mikey.

"Uh? What?" said Norm, distractedly. "Do you want me to leave the room, Mikey?"

"What?" said Mikey. "No, not **that** kind of changing, Norm. I mean, I think I might be **changing**."

"What are you on about, Mikey?"

Norm suddenly snapped out of his trance-like state. "Hormones?"

"I've been doing some research on the net," said Mikey. "Apparently it's quite common."

"What is?"

"To stink," said Mikey. "When you've got hormones."

"Whoa," said Norm, unsure what else to say. This was disturbing news to say the least. He and Mikey had known each other since they were babies. They'd started parent and toddler group on the same day. They'd started school on the same day. They'd been to the same birthday parties as each other.

They'd even been on
holiday together. And
now Mikey was telling
him that he'd got hormones?

"Are you sure?" said Norm.

"That I've got hormones?" said Mikey. "Pretty sure, yeah."

"What else did you find out?" said Norm.

Mikey looked unsure again. "That I might…"

"What?" said Norm.

"Start becoming interested in the opposite…"

Opposite what? thought Norm. Point of view? Side of the road?

"Thingy," said Mikey.

"Thingy?" said Norm.

"Gender."

Norm sighed. What was Mikey doing using all these fancy big words? Unless, of course, that was another sign of having hormones. They made you talk funny.

"**Girls**," said Mikey eventually.

"**Girls?**" said Norm.

"**Girls**," said Mikey.

"Right," said Norm.

The room fell eerily silent. By now the video Norm had been watching had finished. So too had the game of FIFA Mikey had been playing. Outside in the street a car door slammed and a dog barked. Norm briefly wondered whether the two things were connected. Whether the car door had slammed and actually **caused** the dog to bark. But even as he wondered he knew that all he was doing was avoiding thinking about what he should **really** be thinking about. And asking what he should **really** be asking.

"And?"

"And what?" said Mikey.

"Are you?" said Norm.

"Starting to become interested in girls?" said Mikey.

Norm nodded.

"Not yet," said Mikey starting another game of FIFA.

Not yet? thought Norm. Not **yet?** What was **that** supposed to mean? That it was somehow inevitable that Mikey **would** become interested in girls at some stage? That it was only a matter of time? That it was a done deal?

Norm sighed.

"What?" said Mikey.

"Nothing," said Norm, clicking on another biking video.

CHAPTER 5

Norm was off like a shot the second his mum called to say that they'd got back from IKEA. Normally Norm would have been only too happy to stay at Mikey's for longer. Much, **much** longer, in fact. But the truth was the call from his mum had come as something of a relief. And not just because it was lunchtime. There'd been a slightly weird atmosphere ever since the conversation had turned to talk of deodorant and hormones and the opposite thingy. Norm had been looking for an excuse to go and now he'd got one.

Hormones?!!

GIRLS?!

Rather than head straight home though, Norm decided to take a detour and go via the allotments. He wasn't particularly desperate to get home. Far from it. And besides, if he went via the allotments, Norm knew there was a very good chance that he'd see the one person who **_truly_** understood him. And he did.

"Look what the cat's dragged in," said Grandpa, emerging from his shed with a watering can as Norm skidded to a halt and got off his bike.

"Nice to see you too, Grandpa," said Norm.

"To what do I owe the pleasure?"

"Pardon?" said Norm.

"What brings you here?" said Grandpa. "And don't say your bike."

"Nothing," said Norm, a bit **_too_** matter-of-factly. "I was just passing, that's all."

Grandpa raised his cloud-like eyebrows.

"What?" said Norm. "I **was!**"

"I can read you like a book, Norman."

Norm pulled a face. "What kind of book?"

"One with pictures and not many words," said Grandpa.

Norm and Grandpa stared at each other for a few seconds before eventually Grandpa's eyes crinkled ever so slightly in the corners. It was the closest he ever came to smiling.

"Seriously, Norman. I know you haven't come down here just to hang out with me."

Norm looked hurt. "I **might** have done, Grandpa!"

Grandpa looked at Norm. "Have you come down here just to hang out with me?"

"No," said Norm staring at the ground.

"Thought not," said Grandpa. "Get on with it."

Norm said nothing.

"Come on," said Grandpa. "I haven't got all day."

Still Norm said nothing.

"I'm warning you, Norman. If you stand there much longer I'm going to water you."

Norm grinned.

"That's better," said Grandpa. "Now spit it out."

"It's Mikey," said Norm.

"What about him?" said Grandpa.

"He thinks he's changing."

"Does he now?"

"He's got hormones," said Norm.

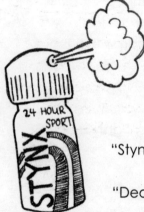

"Has he now? And how do you know that?"

"He told me," said Norm. "He's started to use Stynx."

"Stynx?" said Grandpa.

"Deodorant," said Norm.

Grandpa shook his head and took a sharp intake of breath.

"Deodorant, eh?"

Norm nodded. "He's looked it up on the internet."

"It's the start of the slippery slope, Norman."

"What is?" said Norm. "The internet?"

"Deodorant," said Grandpa. "It's the tip of the iceberg."

What was it with everybody and flipping icebergs today? wondered Norm. That was twice in one day he'd heard that expression. What with that and all those big words Mikey kept coming out with, Norm was beginning to feel like a foreigner in his own country. Like he was Belgian but couldn't speak Belgian. Except of course there was no such language as Belgian. Norm knew that now.

"How old is he?" said Grandpa.

"Thirteen," said Norm.

"Ah, there you go then," said Grandpa. "That explains everything!"

No it flipping doesn't, thought Norm. It didn't explain **anything**, let alone everything! What was Grandpa on about?

"He's older than you."

Norm pulled a face. "Only a *bit*. I'm **nearly** thirteen."

"But, crucially," said Grandpa, "Mikey actually **is** thirteen."

"Yeah, but..."

"It's like flicking a switch."

"What is?" said Norm.

"Turning thirteen," said Grandpa. "It's all downhill after that."

Norm watched as Grandpa began watering some vegetables. He was seriously beginning to wish he'd gone to IKEA after all.

"One day you're dressing up as Spider-Man, the next you prefer pottering about the garden and watching interesting documentaries on TV."

By now Norm was starting to get genuinely worried. This wasn't exactly what he'd come to hear. He'd come to the allotments hoping that Grandpa might actually make him feel **better** – not to learn that his life was about to get even **more** rubbish.

"I remember starting to use deodorant like it was yesterday, Norman," said Grandpa, staring wistfully into the distance. "And look at me now. I'm nearly dead."

Norm and Grandpa looked at each other for a moment before eventually Grandpa's eyes started to crinkle in the corners. Only very slightly. But it was enough.

"Very funny, Grandpa," said Norm. "And I wish you wouldn't say that."

"What?" said Grandpa, stopping watering for a moment.

"That you're nearly dead. "You're nowhere **near** dead!"

"I'm not getting any younger, Norman."

"Obviously," said Norm.

"What's that supposed to mean?" said Grandpa.

"**None** of us are getting any younger!" said Norm. "**I'm** not getting any younger! Brian and Dave aren't getting any younger!"

The conversation was beginning to depress Norm. And he hadn't been feeling particularly chirpy in the first place.

"Grandpa?"

"What?"

"All that stuff about the start of the slippery iceberg and flicking a switch and stuff?"

"What about it?" said Grandpa.

"It was just a joke, right?"

"Of course it was just a..." Grandpa stopped

watering again. "Oh, I see. So *that's* what this is about."

Norm waited for Grandpa to carry on. He wasn't a hundred per cent certain he knew what this was about himself. He was curious to hear what Grandpa had to say.

"You're wondering whether *you're* about to change too, aren't you?

Was he? thought Norm. He wasn't aware that he was.

"This isn't about Mikey at all, is it?" said Grandpa.

Isn't it? thought Norm. He'd *thought* it was.

"This is about you, isn't it, Norman?"

Is it? thought Norm.

"I might have known," said Grandpa.

Grandpa put down the watering can and beckoned for Norm to follow him towards the shed.

"Take a seat," said Grandpa, plonking himself down on an old wooden chair.

Norm looked around but couldn't see anything else to sit on.

"The bucket," said Grandpa, with a tilt of his head.

Norm pulled a face. How was he supposed to sit on a bucket? He'd get stuck.

"Turn it upside down," said Grandpa, as if he'd been reading Norm's mind.

"Oh right," said Norm, doing as Grandpa suggested.

"**Now** sit on it."

Norm sat down on the upturned bucket and waited. He just hoped that whatever Grandpa was about to say wouldn't take too long – or contain too many biological details.

"Hormones aren't like germs, you know, Norman."

"What do you mean?" said Norm.

"You don't **catch** hormones," said Grandpa. "They're not contagious."

"Really?" said Norm.

"Of course not," said Grandpa. "They're just chemicals. We've all got them."

Whoa, thought Norm. He had chemicals? Was that legal?

"You've got them. Your brothers have got them. Your parents have got them."

That was it, thought Norm. There was a line. And Grandpa had just crossed it. The thought that he had hormones himself was bad enough. But his parents? Surely not?

"Did you say my **parents** have got hormones?"

"Of course," said Grandpa. "If they didn't then you wouldn't be here."

"You mean the allotments?" said Norm.

Grandpa sighed. "I mean you wouldn't have been **born**, you dipstick."

"Oh," said Norm, immediately wishing he hadn't asked.

"I've still got one or two knocking about myself, somewhere," said Grandpa.

"One or two what?" said Norm.

"Hormones," said Grandpa.

"Right," said Norm, again wishing he hadn't asked.

"Only one or two, mind," said Grandpa, getting up. "Talking of which, don't want to be late for my date."

But Norm wasn't listening any more. He had enough on his plate already. Much more of this and he was going to throw up. He'd have even more on his plate then.

CHAPTER 6

"What do **you** want?" said Norm as soon as he heard the tell-tale creak of the tell-tale creaky floorboard.

"How did you know it was me?" said Brian.

"I didn't," said Norm, without bothering to look up from the computer. "Do now, though."

"Oh, I see," said Brian. "Very clever, Norman."

"Thanks," said Norm, like he couldn't care less. Which he couldn't. "Now, if that's all you came here to say, you can clear off again."

"Actually, that's not what I came here to say," said Brian.

Norm turned round and looked at his middle brother, who, he could now see, was grinning in an extremely annoying manner. Annoying even by Brian's standards. And when it came to being annoying, Brian had **extremely** high standards.

"Don't keep me in suspense, Brian. I'm on the edge of my seat here."

"I know you were in there."

"In where?" said Norm.

"The bathroom," said Brian. "Before we went to IKEA. I know you were in there."

"Prove it," said Norm.

"The window was open when we got back," said Brian.

"Yeah, so?" said Norm.

"The toothbrushes had been knocked over."

"Yeah, so?" said Norm, beginning to get
more and more wound up.

"There were footprints on
the windowsill."

"Yeah, so?" snapped Norm.

"They were **your** footprints,
Norman," said Brian. "They
matched your trainers."

Norm pulled a face. "How do you know?"

"I've checked."

"You've checked?" said Norm. "You've actually
checked?"

"Course I have," said Brian.

Norm sighed. What kind of freak would actually
go to the bother of **doing** that? Flipping Brian,
that was who!

"You need to get a life while stocks last," muttered Norm darkly.

"No I don't," said Brian.
"I've already got one, thanks."

"Let's just suppose you're right."

They looked at each other for a moment. It was long enough though. Norm knew that Brian knew he was right. Furthermore, Brian *knew* that Norm knew that he knew he was right.

"What are you going to do about it?" said Norm menacingly.

Brian grinned again. "Already have."

"What do you mean?" said Norm. "What are you talking about?"

"I mean I already **have** done something about it," said Brian.

"You have?" said Norm, not quite so menacingly. "What?"

"I told Dad."

"What?" said Norm again.

"I told Dad," said Brian.

"Why?" said Norm.

Brian shrugged. "Felt like it."

Norm sighed. "You *felt* like it?"

"Yeah," said Brian. "I just felt like it."

Norm glared at Brian like an eagle eyeing up a rabbit. "What did he say?"

Brian thought for a second. "Actually, he seemed more bothered about you leaving the window open than anything else."

"What, so he didn't care about me going to Mikey's instead of IKEA?"

"Not really, no," said Brian. "I think it was more the fact that you were wasting energy."

Figures, thought Norm. But as far as Norm was concerned, going to IKEA would have been a far greater waste of energy than leaving a flipping window open ever would be.

"I suppose he started banging on about global warming?"

"He did, actually," said Brian.

"And I presume he said it was all my fault?"

"Yeah," said Brian. "How do you know that?"

"Just a wild guess," said Norm, who by now had turned back to the computer and was busy googling.

Even though he knew there was absolutely no chance of actually *getting* a new bike in the near future. Or the future, full flipping stop for that matter. But there was no harm looking. And dreaming. And drooling.

"Dad says he wants to see you, by the way, Norman."

"Ooh, I'm scared," said Norm.

"Really?" said Brian.

"No, not really," said Norm, without taking his eyes off the screen.

"Oh, I see," said Brian. "You're being sarcastic."

Norm couldn't be bothered replying. The only thing Norm was even remotely bothered about was currently staring him smack in the face. The fact that he'd never be able to afford a bike like that in a gazillion years was neither here nor there.

"Sarcasm is the lowest form of humour," said Brian.

"Are you still here?" said Norm.

Brian pulled a face. "Are you being sarcastic again? I can't tell."

Norm sighed and turned round.

"Brian?"

"What?"

"Clear off, you little freak. And before you ask, no. I'm flipping **not** being sarcastic."

Norm might have known this would have no effect. Telling Brian to go away was a bit like telling the tide not to come in.

"Why are you not scared?"

"Because he's all talk, that's why," said Norm.

"Who?" said Brian. "Dad?"

"He's all hot air."

"What do you mean?" said Brian.

"He never carries out any threats," said Norm.

"Really?" said Brian. "I haven't noticed."

"That's because he never flipping threatens **you**, Brian!"

"Yeah, he does!"

"When?" snorted Norm. "When did Dad last threaten **you?**"

Brian thought for a moment.

"Last week."

"Last week?"

"Yeah," said Brian. "He said if I didn't eat all my greens I wouldn't get any pudding."

Norm couldn't help laughing. That was Brian's idea of a threat? It was almost as laughable as Mikey's mum's so-called "wobbly"!

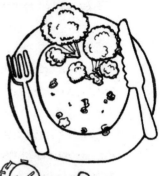

"And did you?"

"Did I what?" said Brian.

"Eat all your greens?" said Norm.

"No."

"Did you still get pudding?"

"Yeah," said Brian.

"There you go!" said Norm. "That's **exactly** what I mean! He's full of hot air!"

"Who is?" said a voice.

Norm didn't need to turn round to know that it was his dad. But he still did.

"Oh, hi, Dad."

How long had he been there? wondered Norm. More importantly, how much had he heard?

"Who is?" repeated Norm's dad.

"Oh, just this kid Brian knows," said Norm. "Isn't that right, Brian?"

"What?" said Brian.

"This kid you know," said Norm, glaring at Brian like a great white shark eyeing up a sardine.

"Oh yeah," said Brian.

Norm's dad turned to Brian expectantly. "What's his name?"

"Ryan O'Toole," blurted Brian.

Norm pulled a face. Rhino Tool? Brian could've made up any name he wanted and his dad wouldn't have known any different. Was that really the best he could come up with? **Rhino Tool?** That wasn't even a proper name. It was an animal followed by the first random word Brian had thought of. Like Turtle Carpet. Or Badger Cheese.

"I see," said Norm's dad. "And why is he full of hot air, Norman?"

"Because, erm..."

Because what? thought Norm. He needed to think on his feet here. Well, strictly speaking he needed to think on his backside as he was still sat down.

"Because he's always letting these really disgusting far..."

"I get the picture," said Norm's dad holding a hand up. "Can I have a word please, Norman?"

"Go crazy, Dad. Have two," said Norm.

"Downstairs," said Norm's dad, disappearing.

"Oh, right," said Norm, getting up from the computer.

"I'll keep your seat warm," said Brian, sitting down.

"Don't **X** out of th—" began Norm.

But it was too late. Brian had already closed the site Norm had been looking at. Norm hadn't even got round to adding the bike to the list of bikes he'd never get.

"Thanks **very** much, Brian," said Norm.

"Don't mention it," said Brian.

"Norman?" called Norm's dad from the foot of the stairs.

"Coming, Dad!" said Norm.

CHAPTER 7

Norm walked into the lounge to find not only his dad already sat on the sofa but his mum as well. This was not normally a good sign in Norm's experience. This was normally a **bad** sign in Norm's experience. And when it came to bad signs, Norm had had **plenty** of experience.

"Sit down, love," said Norm's mum, patting a space between them and causing a cloud of dust to rise and swirl about in the air like an ash cloud from a tiny volcano.

Norm sat down, not on the sofa but in an armchair. The one nearest the door. He wanted to be able to make a swift exit if necessary.

Norm's dad exhaled noisily, making a sound like a whoopee cushion with his lips. "We need to talk."

"Do we, Dad?" said Norm, nonchalantly.

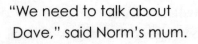

"We need to talk about Dave," said Norm's mum.

Dave? thought Norm. He'd assumed this was going to be a lecture about the importance of closing windows. What did they need to talk about Dave for?

"What about him?" said Norm.

"Have you not noticed?" said Norm's dad.

Not noticed **what?** thought Norm. What kind of stupid question was that? How was he supposed to know what he hadn't noticed? That was the whole point of not noticing something!

"We think he's been acting a little..." began Norm's mum.

"What?" said Norm.

"Not **what**," said Norm's dad. "**Pardon**."

"I meant, he's been acting a little **what?**" said Norm.

"Strangely," said Norm's mum.

Strangely? thought Norm. Dave hadn't been **acting** strangely. Dave was strange. OK so probably not **quite** as strange as Brian. Then again, thought Norm, when it came to strangeness, Brian was in a class of his own. In fact, never mind a **class** of his own – when it came to strangeness Brian had the whole flipping school to himself.

"We lost him in IKEA for a while just now," said Norm's dad. "When we found him again he was fast asleep in the bedroom department."

Norm certainly couldn't blame Dave for falling asleep in IKEA. The mere thought of going there was enough to set Norm off yawning. And if you were going to fall asleep anywhere, thought Norm, it might as well be in the bedroom department. Better than falling asleep in the kitchen department anyway.

"Something's not quite right," said Norm's mum. "He's just not himself."

Norm didn't reply immediately. He was busy thinking. Normally Dave would have gone bananas if Norm had suddenly burst into the bathroom and dropped his trousers. But he hadn't made a peep. He'd even been happy to take the rap for being in the bathroom so long. He'd actively encouraged Norm to skedaddle. Yes, now his mum came to mention it, Dave **had** been acting pretty strangely.

"What do you want me to do about it?" said Norm.

"We want you to find out what the matter is," said Norm's mum.

"Uh?" said Norm. "How am I supposed to do that?"

"Talk to him."

"**Talk** to him?" said Norm like his mum had just suggested he stripped naked and ran down the street playing the bagpipes. "Actually **talk** to him?"

"Why not?" replied Norm's mum with a shrug of her shoulders. "He's your brother, isn't he?"

Yes, thought Norm. And that was exactly **why** he didn't want to talk to Dave any more than he abso-flipping-lutely **had** to. Besides, he'd never actually seen the paperwork. And until he had, Norm only had his parents' word for it that he and his brothers were biologically related.

"He looks up to you, love."

Norm pulled a face. "Well, he would, Mum. He's shorter than me."

Norm's mum smiled. "I mean you're a role model for him."

Norm's dad made another whoopee cushion sound. "Heaven help him."

And what was **that** supposed to mean? thought Norm.

"Please?" said Norm's mum. "For us?"

Norm really hated it when his parents did that. **For us?** Didn't Norm do enough *for them* already? Were they trying to make him feel guilty or something? Because if they were, they could flipping well forget it!

"Do it however you want," said Norm's dad. "Do it on Facebook for all I care."

"Alan," said Norm's mum disapprovingly.

"What?" said Norm's dad.

"You know Dave's too young to be on Facebook."

Not
according to
his latest profile
he's not, thought
Norm. Last time
he'd looked, Dave was
thirty-nine and a successful businessman with a
Ferrari and a yacht in the Caribbean.

"Text him, then," said Norm's dad.

Norm's mum sighed in exasperation. "I don't
believe it."

Neither do I, thought Norm. He had no intention
of wasting a perfectly good text on his stupid little
brother.

"Norman?" said Norm's mum.

Norm looked at his mum. He recognised that
change in tone of voice. It meant his mum meant
business. It meant she was **not** to be messed with.

"Yes, Mum?"

"Just do it."

There was a sudden commotion outside. It sounded like they were about to have company.

"I'll pay you," said Norm's dad quickly.

"What?" said Norm's mum in amazement.

"I said I'll pay him."

"For talking to his own brother?"

"If it means getting to the root of the problem, yes," said Norm's dad.

But at that moment the door suddenly burst open and in rushed John and Dave. Norm still hadn't got used to there being a dog in the house. He'd still not entirely got used to having **brothers** in the house, let alone a flipping dog. Let alone a dog named after Grandpa's favourite member of The Beatles. It wouldn't have been so bad, but Norm was pretty sure Grandpa had meant it to be called Lennon – not John.

As if sensing what Norm was thinking, John launched himself through the air, like a furry guided missile, hitting his intended target with unerring accuracy.

"Get off me!" yelled Norm, forgetting that John's first language was Polish. Not that it would have made any difference if Norm **had** remembered. He didn't know what the Polish for **get off me** was, anyway.

Not only did John **not** get off Norm, he proceeded to lick him full in the face like Norm was some kind of cat-flavoured lollipop. It felt to Norm like he was being smothered by a jellyfish. Not that Norm had ever actually been smothered by a jellyfish before. But he imagined that's what it would have felt like.

As for the smell of John's breath? It was like **nothing** Norm had ever smelt before – or ever wanted to smell again for that matter.

"**Ugh!**" said Norm, gasping for air. "**That** is **disgusting!**"

"I tried to stop him but he didn't understand," said Dave.

"Stop him what?" said Norm's dad.

"Drinking from the toilet," said Dave.

If Norm hadn't already felt like throwing up, he did now. There was a part of him that wanted to know whether the toilet had been flushed. On the other hand there was a part of him that didn't. If Norm's dad had been the last one in the bathroom then the answer was probably no! His dad only flushed **when necessary!** Well from now on, thought Norm, **every** flipping time was going to be **necessary!**

"Why don't you two take John for a walk?" said Norm's mum, exchanging a quick glance with Norm's dad.

"What?" said Norm's dad, not immediately twigging. "Oh yes. Good idea. Off you go, boys!"

John had already disengaged himself from Norm's face – **walk** being one of the few English words he actually understood – and trotted off in search of his lead. The bad news, as far as Norm was concerned, was that he abso-flipping-lutely **hated** walks. Walks, as far as Norm was concerned, were like chips without ketchup.  Completely pointless. The good news was, at least Norm could breathe again.

"Don't forget now, Norman," said Norm's dad. "I'll pay you."

"How much?" said Norm.

"Ten pounds?"

"Ten pounds?" squeaked Dave. "For walking the dog?"

Norm looked at his little brother. He couldn't very well tell him the **real** reason his dad was offering to pay him.

"We'll split it."

"Really?" said Dave. "Thanks."

"You'll do it, then?" said Norm's mum.

"Do what?" said Norm.

"Go for a **walk?**" said Norm's dad, winking.

Norm sighed. A tenner was a tenner in any language. Except Belgian.

"Well?" said Norm's mum expectantly.

"Oh, what the heck," said Norm.

"Language," said Dave.

CHAPTER 8

"So when do I get my fiver, then?" said Dave.

Norm turned to his youngest brother and laughed. "Fiver? Who said anything about a **_fiver?_**"

They were heading for the park. They would probably have reached it by now too if John hadn't stopped to pee on every available lamppost and every available wheelie bin.

"**_You_** did," said Dave.

"No I didn't," said Norm.

"Yeah you did."

"No I didn't."

"I think you'll find you did."

"I think you'll find I didn't."

This, thought Norm, could well go on for some time. When Dave decided that he was right about something, boy did he decide that he was right about something. Once he dug his heels in, that was that. Game, set and flipping match. Everyone else might as well pack up and go home. The greatest scientific minds in the world could conclude once and for all that the chicken came before the egg, but if Dave decided it was the other way round? It was the other way round. End of.

"You said you'd split the money."

Norm nodded. "True."

"Well?" said Dave.

Norm knew exactly what Dave was getting at. He was just enjoying making him say it out loud. "Well what?"

"Half of ten pounds is a fiver," said Dave. "50/50."

Norm smiled in preparation for delivering the killer blow. "Who said anything about 50/50?"

Dave's face dropped like a parachutist without a parachute. It was practically unheard of for him to lose an argument. Norm briefly considered whipping his phone out to take a picture.

"But..."

"But what?" said Norm, still smiling.

"That's not fair."

Norm snorted. "Welcome to my world, Dave!"

said a voice.

Norm and Dave turned round to find John peeing on a parked police car. Could've been worse, thought Norm. Could've been a parked policeman.

"Sorry, officer," said Dave, giving John's lead a sharp tug and pulling him away. "He's Polish."

The policeman looked distinctly puzzled.

"Not me," said Norm. "He means the dog."

"Are you being funny?" said the policeman.

Norm thought for a moment. Was he? "I don't think so. Not on purpose anyway."

The policeman didn't look convinced. "Hmm, well, mind how you go."

"We will, officer," said Dave.

They walked on in silence – Dave contemplating his next move; Norm thinking what a stupid thing that was to have said. What did the policeman mean, "Mind how you go"? What? Like they **wouldn't** have minded how they'd gone if he **hadn't** said that?

"So?" said Dave once he'd finished contemplating.

"So what?" said Norm.

"How much were you thinking of giving me?"

Norm stroked his chin thoughtfully. "Hmm, let me see now. How does a pound sound?"

"Seriously?" said Dave. "One pound?"

Norm nodded.

"It sounds rubbish."

Norm had been half expecting this. More than half expecting it actually. More like three quarters expecting it. He knew that Dave wouldn't take it lying down. He knew he'd try to barter. He knew that **he'd** have done exactly the same if he was Dave. Which thankfully he wasn't. Who wanted to be seven again? Barely out of nappies? Watching TV programmes featuring grown-ups prancing about in oversized costumes singing stupid songs? Having to go to bed ten minutes after you've got up? What kind of futile existence was that?

On the other hand, thought Norm – being the centre of the universe? Being biologically incapable of ever doing anything wrong? Never being blamed for wasting money or global flipping warming? The more Norm thought about it, the more he thought that perhaps being Dave wouldn't be **quite** such a bad thing after all.

"Three quid," said Dave.

"No way!" said Norm. "One-fifty."

"Two pounds."

Norm thought for a moment. "Deal."

"Should just about be enough," said Dave absent-mindedly.

"Enough for what?"

Dave appeared to hesitate.

"Can of Stynx."

Uh? thought Norm. What did Dave need deodorant for? Surely *he* wasn't changing as well, was he? Was that why he'd been in the bath earlier?

"Stynx?" said Norm. "You're only seven!"

"I know perfectly well how old I am, Norman," said Dave. "I'm not stupid!"

"I never said you were," said Norm, conscious not to get into another pointless argument. They'd be here all day and most of the flipping night at this rate!

Norm looked at his little brother. All was clearly not well in Daveland. Even Norm could see that. "What's up, little bruv?"

Dave hesitated again. "I'm not sure I should say."

"Not sure you should say what?" said Norm.

Dave glanced at Norm and for a brief moment looked as if he was about to smile. "Nice try, Norman."

"Seriously, Dave. Are you going to tell me what's going on, or what?"

Dave shrugged. "Or what?"

"What?" said Norm.

"Or **what**, what?" said Dave.

Norm was beginning to get confused.

"Have Mum and Dad asked you to ask me?" said Dave.

"Ask you what?" said Norm, already beginning to feel his cheeks redden.

"What the matter is?" said Dave. "With me, I mean."

You had to hand it to Dave, thought Norm. He was good. He was **flipping** good. Yes, he could be unbelievably annoying at times. And at other times he could be stubborn beyond belief. But for a seven-year-old, he could also be incredibly shrewd.

"Well?" said Dave. "Have they?"

"No!" said Norm. "What makes you think that?"

"Two things," said Dave. "Firstly, you couldn't normally care less if anything was up. Secondly, you wouldn't normally call me 'little bruv'."

"Yeah, well – you know," said Norm, unable to think what else to say. Dave knew. And furthermore, Dave knew that Norm knew he knew.

By now they'd reached the park. The first thing John did after he was let off the lead was to run up to a bench and pee on it. The couple sitting on the bench and eating a picnic were not amused.

"Oh, I get it!" said Dave.

Uh-oh, thought Norm. What exactly did Dave get?

"That's what the money's for, isn't it? It's not for taking John for a walk."

"Maybe," mumbled Norm.

"It *is*," said Dave. "You're being paid to find out what the matter with me is, aren't you, Norman?"

This was getting uncanny, thought Norm. How did Dave do it?

"I'll tell you if you want."

"Really?" said Norm. "Just like that?"

Dave nodded. "Just like that. But you've got to promise not to tell anybody."

Norm thought for a moment. What should he do here? The whole point was that he had to find out the matter was and then report back to his parents. And now Dave was getting him to promise not to tell them?

"But..."

"Just make something up," said Dave.

"What?" said Norm.

"Just make something up."

Norm hadn't thought of that. But he did now. And it wasn't such a bad idea. In fact, thinking about it, it was a pretty flipping **good** idea. He could just make something up to tell his parents. He'd get his hands on the dosh and they'd be none the wiser. And let's face it, thought Norm, they weren't too wise in the first place. Brilliant. Dave had done it again!

"Let's go," said Norm, turning round and heading for home.

"But..." began Dave.

"What?" said Norm.

"Don't you want to know what's wrong with me?"

Norm pulled a face. "Not particularly, no."

"But..."

"I'm just going to make something up."

"But..."

"What?" snapped Norm impatiently.

Dave hesitated. "Maybe I *want* to tell you."

Norm suddenly remembered what his mum had said. About Dave looking up to him. About Norm being a role model, whatever **that** meant! Perhaps he ought to let Dave say what he wanted to say. Let him get it off his chest. Then maybe he'd shut up.

"Go on, then," said Norm. "But get a move on."

"I'm being bullied," said Dave, matter-of-factly.

Norm stopped dead in his tracks. "That's horrible!"

"It's immoral, **that's** what it is," said Dave.

"What?" said Norm. "No. **That's** horrible!"

Dave looked where Norm was pointing to see John sniffing another dog's bum – and another dog sniffing John's bum.

"It's perfectly natural," said Dave.

Norm pulled a face. "You call *that* natural?"

"For a dog it is, yeah."

In that case, thought Norm, thank goodness he wasn't a flipping dog. Drinking from toilets was gross enough. But sniffing other dogs' backsides? It didn't bear thinking about. Which was slightly unfortunate because now Norm *had* just thought about it.

"So what are you going to do?" said Dave.

Norm snorted derisively. "I'm not going to do anything!"

"About me being bullied."

Norm turned to Dave.

"You're being bullied?"

"I knew you weren't listening!" said Dave. "*That's* what the matter is, Norman! I'm being bullied!"

"Whoa," said Norm.

"That's what I need the can of Stynx for."

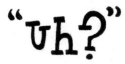

Norm was confused. What was Dave going to do with a can of Stynx? Hit someone over the head with it?

"They say I've got to give them a can of Stynx Or else."

"Or else what?"

Dave shrugged. "I don't know. Just – or *else*"

"Who's **they**, Dave?"

Dave shuffled about and stared at the ground. "Can't say."

"What do you mean, you can't say?"

"I mean I **can** say. But I'd rather **not** say."

"Why not?" said Norm.

"Why would I rather not say?" said Dave.

"Yeah."

Dave did a bit more shuffling and staring at the ground.

"I'd rather not say."

Norm sighed. This was getting ridiculous. "You'd rather not say why you'd rather not say?"

"Yeah," said Dave.

"Why not?"

"I just wouldn't!" said Dave, clearly agitated.

Norm looked at Dave. No wonder he didn't seem himself. He was being bullied. Norm didn't like it. He didn't like it one little bit. In fact the more Norm thought about it, the angrier he got. How dare they? How flipping dare they? Whoever **they** were. Dave was his brother. **He** could bully him if he wanted. But no one else could. That was out of flipping order, that was!

Norm sighed. He couldn't believe it. Even though his brothers drove him

abso-flipping-lutely

mad at times, the thought of someone **else** being horrible to them made him even madder. Underneath it all, Norm actually felt very protective towards Dave and Brian. It was so flipping unfair.

"What's the matter?" said Dave.

"What?" said Norm. "Nothing. I was just thinking, that's all."

"What about?"

"I'd rather not say," said Norm.

CHAPTER 9

"So?" said Norm's mum as Norm walked through the door. "Did you manage to find anything out, love? About Dave I mean?"

"Erm, well..." began Norm.

"Wait," said Norm's dad. "Before you tell us, stick the kettle on."

"'Kay, Dad," said Norm, heading for the kitchen and grateful for the distraction. He still hadn't decided what he was going to say to his parents. He hadn't actually **promised** Dave that he wouldn't tell them about him being bullied. But he knew that he couldn't. It wouldn't be fair. Especially after Dave had saved him from going to IKEA.

Hang on, thought Norm. What was **he** doing, worrying about doing something that wasn't fair? Him – Norm – of **all** people? He was the last person on earth who should worry about doing something to somebody **else** that wasn't flipping fair! Especially one of his flipping brothers! He wouldn't think twice about it normally. So why was he thinking about it now? What was going on? Was it his hormones? Was he changing? Was Norm's world as he knew it about to end?

Norm stared out the kitchen window as he turned the tap on and filled the kettle up. Brian and Dave were playing football in the garden. So too was John, until he wandered off and peed on a garden gnome. Instinctively, Norm chuckled. Which was good actually, thinking about it, thought Norm. Because if he still found the sight of a dog peeing on a garden gnome essentially funny, then maybe he wasn't changing just yet after all.

"You coming, love?" yelled Norm's mum from the front room.

"Just a minute!" yelled Norm, turning the tap off – and the kettle on.

"We thought you'd got lost," said Norm's dad a few moments later, when Norm reappeared in the doorway.

Lost? thought Norm. In a house this small? No chance. At least in their old house there'd been room to swing a cat. Not that they ever did, of course. How could they? They didn't have a cat.

"So?" said Norm's mum. "What have you got to tell us?"

Good point, thought Norm. What *had* he got to tell his parents? He **still** hadn't decided. He was in dire need of some sudden inspiration.

"He's worried about Grandpa," said Norm, glancing at a photo on the mantelpiece. It was an old black-and-white photo of someone in a skinny suit with a pudding-bowl haircut, grinning cheesily and giving a thumbs-up to the camera. It could almost have

been one of The
Beatles. But it wasn't.
It was unmistakably
Grandpa.

"Grandpa?" said
Norm's mum. "Why's
he worried about
Grandpa, love?"

Norm puffed his cheeks
out. "Dunno. I think he's afraid he's going to..."

Norm didn't finish the sentence. He didn't need to.

"Die?" said Norm's dad.

"Thank you, Alan," said Norm's mum pointedly, giving
Norm's dad a thin-lipped smile.

"Well," said Norm's dad. "We're all going to die
eventually."

Norm's mum sighed. "Yes. **Eventually**."

"So what's the problem?"

"He's **seven**," said Norm's mum. "And there are some things you just don't need to know when you're seven."

Norm pulled a face. He was beginning to wish he'd made up something else instead. Something about Dave wetting his bed maybe? Dave's own bed, that is. Not Norm's.

"Norman," said Norm's mum in her not-to-be-messed-with voice.

"Yes, Mum?"

"Grandpa is **not** going to die, all right?"

Norm nodded.

"Not for a very long time, anyway."

"As far as we know," added Norm's dad.

"Alan!" said Norm's mum.

"Sorry," said Norm's dad.

"He is *not* going to die, Norman!"

"Who isn't?" said Dave.

Norm turned round to find not only his little brother standing in the doorway, but also his middle brother, together with John the dog. How much had they heard? Did it matter if they **had** heard? Grandpa **wasn't** going to die. That was a **good** thing.

"John," said Norm, just to be on the safe side.

Brian immediately looked horrified. "What?"

"John's not going to die," said Norm.

"I know he's not," said Brian.

"Not for ages anyway," added Dave.

Brian covered up John's ears with his hands. "Don't listen to them, John."

"He can't understand you," said Dave. "He's Polish."

"Yeah," said Norm. "And he's a dog."

Norm's mum sighed. "We weren't talking about John. We were talking about Grandpa."

"I knew it," said Dave.

Norm looked at Dave. He *knew* he knew it. "So that's good, isn't it?"

"What is?" said Dave.

"That Grandpa's not going to die."

Dave pulled a face. "What?"

Norm glared at Dave, trying hard to get him to read his mind. This was what he'd told Mum and Dad. This was what Dave was supposed to be worried about. There was the briefest of pauses whilst the penny dropped.

"Oh, right, yeah!" said Dave. "That's great news!"

Norm's mum smiled. "And even better than that, he's coming to babysit tomorrow night!"

"Yeah!" sang Brian and Dave together.

"Even better?" said Norm.

"Pardon, love?" said Norm's mum.

"Grandpa coming to babysit is even better than him not dying?"

"Just trying to change the subject," said Norm's mum in her not-to-be-messed-with voice and smiling another thin-lipped smile.

"Let's see how that kettle's getting on, shall we?" said Norm's dad, getting up and heading for the kitchen.

CHAPTER 10

The kettle, as it turned out, was getting on just fine. Which was more than could be said for Norm's dad when he saw it.

"Norman?"

"What?" said Norm, appearing in the kitchen a moment or so later.

The vein on the side of Norm's dad's head had already begun to throb. Not that Norm noticed.

"What do you mean, **what?**"

Norm was genuinely puzzled. What part of **what** did his dad not understand?

"Can you not see?"

This was getting weirder by the second, thought Norm. He had no idea what it was that he was supposed to be seeing – let alone whether he could actually see it or not.

"Well?" said Norm's dad, getting more and more exasperated.

"Sorry, Dad, you're going to have to give me a clue," said Norm.

Norm's dad sighed. "Two words. Global warming."

Seven words, thought Norm. What was his dad flipping on about?

"What did I tell you to do a few minutes ago?"

Norm thought for a moment.

"I told you to put the kettle on."

So if he knew, why flipping ask? thought Norm.

"Well?" said Norm's dad.

Was this a trick question? wondered Norm. "I did, Dad."

"I can see that, Norman!" said Norm's dad. "And do you know **why** I can see that?"

"No, Dad."

"It still hasn't boiled!"

Norm looked. Sure enough, the kettle was making a kind of low whooshing sound.

"Maybe there's a problem, Dad."

Norm's dad looked as if he himself was about to boil. "I'll tell you what the problem is, Norman! You filled it up too full! *That's* what the problem is!"

Norm furrowed his brow. He really couldn't see what all the fuss was. In the great scheme of things, filling the kettle up too full seemed about as serious as running out of custard creams. OK, bad choice, thought Norm. Running out of custard creams actually **was** serious. Some other kind of biscuit then. Rich teas, possibly. But there was no stopping his dad now. He was on a roll.

"Do **you** drink tea or coffee, Norman?"

"No, Dad."

"Do your **brothers** drink tea or coffee?"

"No, Dad."

"So as far as this family's concerned, only your mum and I actually drink tea or coffee."

Gordon flipping Bennet, thought Norm, wishing his dad would hurry up and cut to the chase. He was desperate to go online and check Facebook. He hadn't been in front of a screen since time began. Well – just after lunch anyway. And that was at least two hours ago.

"Well?" said Norm's dad.

"Well what?" said Norm.

"Why did you fill the kettle up?"

"Because it was empty?"

Norm's dad did the
whoopee cushion thing
with his lips again.

"I **mean**, why did you fill it all
the way up?"

Norm shrugged. "Dunno. Just did."

"You just did."

Norm nodded. It was true. He hadn't done it
deliberately. He hadn't **planned** to do it. He just
had. Why was his dad making such a big deal
about it?

"Only fill a kettle with as much water as you actually
need, Norman!"

"'Kay, Dad, whatever," said Norm.

"No, Norman!" said Norm's dad. "**Not** whatever! I really wish you wouldn't say that! Just do as I tell you! Don't overfill the kettle!"

Whatever, thought Norm.

"If you boil more water than you need, it wastes energy!"

Norm knew what was coming next.

"And money!"

"Talking of money..." said Norm.

Norm's dad knew what was coming next.

"Yes?"

"You owe me a tenner for 'walking the dog'," said Norm, making speech marks in the air with his fingers.

"Are you serious?"

Norm shrugged. Was he serious? Flipping right he was serious!

"You leave the TV on standby? You leave lights on? You leave doors open? You flush the toilet when it isn't necessary? You overfill the kettle? And *I* owe *you* money?"

Correct, thought Norm.

There was a pause while Norm's dad weighed up the situation.

"I'll do it this time," he said eventually. "But only because you said you'd split it with Dave."

Norm grinned. It was a good job his dad didn't know *how* he was going to split it.

Norm's dad eyed Norm suspiciously. "You *are* going to do it *fairly*, aren't you?"

"Dad?" said Norm, doing his best to sound as hurt as possible. "How could you even *say* that?"

"Hmm," said Norm's dad. "I'm not happy, Norman."

Really? thought Norm. Now his dad knew how **he** flipping felt then, didn't he?

"I'm telling you. You'd better pull your socks up, or else!"

Or else what? thought Norm. Or else absolutely nothing, probably. Same as usual. And what had pulling socks up got to do with anything, anyway? Did that save flipping energy too?

"Here," said Norm's dad, fishing in his pocket for a ten-pound note and handing it to Norm.

"Thanks, Dad," said Norm, heading for the stairs.

CHAPTER 11

Norm sat down at the computer and signed into Facebook. Mikey was already waiting to chat.

where u bin?

im fine thanks how ru?
typed Norm.

Mikey's reply appeared almost immediately. If he'd sensed that Norm was being sarcastic, he didn't let on.

that conversashun?

wich 1?

the embaracing 1?

Mikey might have been changing, but his spelling remained as bad as ever. Worse even than Norm's. And that was saying something.

```
the 1 bout stynx?
```

yeh

```
wot about it?
```

its confidenshal

```
wot?
```

dont want eny1 else 2 no

```
why not?
```

Mikey didn't reply. At least not straightaway. Not that Norm noticed. The only thing Norm noticed was that he'd just received a friend request from someone called Ryan O'Toole.

Ryan O'Toole? thought Norm. Why did that name look vaguely familiar? But before he knew it, another random thought had popped into Norm's head, without being invited. Dave was being bullied for deodorant – and Mikey had started to use deodorant. Surely the two things weren't connected? Were they? No, thought Norm. Course they weren't. Mikey bully Dave? Not in a squillion, gazillion years. Mikey didn't have a single bad bone in his body. Which was really flipping annoying, thought Norm. But that was another story altogether. No, it was just a coincidence that was all. Norm felt guilty even thinking it.

As Norm continued to stare at the screen, Mikey's reply eventually appeared.

jus dont

`whatever`
shrugged Norm as he typed. Not that Mikey could actually see him shrug.

No sooner had Norm pressed send than another message instantly appeared.

seen chelsea lately?

Oops, thought Norm, remembering that Chelsea had asked him to say hi to Mikey when he'd seen her earlier on. Not that he felt bad or anything. Why should he do what Chelsea wanted him to do? She was so flipping annoying.

```
yeah
```
typed Norm.

```
and? wot?
```

did she say enything?

```
yeah
```

wot?

Norm sighed. What was this? Twenty flipping questions or something? Because if it was, Mikey only had a couple left.

```
she sed 2 say hi
```

2me?

```
yeah 2 you!!!!!!!
```

typed Norm. Who cared who said what? What was the big flipping deal? What did Mikey want to know for?

enything else?

Gordon flipping Bennet! thought Norm, rapidly running out of what little patience he had in the first place. But before he could reply again he heard the tell-tale sound of the tell-tale creaky floorboard...

"And you can clear off, you flipping freak!"

snapped Norm without bothering to turn round.

"Charming," said Grandpa.

Norm swivelled round.

"Oh sorry, Grandpa. I thought it was Brian."

"I should hope so too," said Grandpa, his eyes crinkling ever so slightly in the corners.

"What are you doing here?" said Norm.

"Can't a guy drop by and visit his grandchildren when he feels like it?"

Norm pulled a face. "Grandpa?"

"What?"

"You never just drop by."

"Good point," said Grandpa. "I don't, do I?"

"So?" said Norm. "Why are you here? No offence or anything."

"I've come to babysit."

"Uh?" said Norm. "I thought that was supposed to be tomorrow night"

"It was," said Grandpa. "But something cropped up. I thought I'd come today instead."

Norm studied Grandpa for a moment, checking for signs of any further eye crinkling. But there didn't seem to be any. Grandpa appeared to be deadly serious.

"But…"

"What?" said Grandpa.

"My mum and dad aren't going out tonight."

"They are now," said Grandpa.

Right on cue, Norm's mum called up the stairs.

"You up there, love?"

"Yes, Mum!" replied Norm.

"Your dad and I are just popping out to IKEA for a bit, OK?"

IKEA? thought Norm. Surely not again? They'd only been earlier that day! What could they possibly need now?

"OK, love?"

"'Kay, Mum!" called Norm.

"We won't be long!"

Norm didn't reply. He was still trying to make sense of what he'd just heard. A babysitter had turned up out of the blue. His mum and dad had a sudden and unexpected opportunity to go out. They could have gone anywhere and done anything. The world was their lobster or whatever that expression was. And where were they going? Flipping IKEA, that was where! It was so depressing, thought Norm. Was that really his parents' idea of a good night out? Wandering round looking at flat-pack furniture? Would that be his idea of a good night out when he was their age? If it was, then Norm now knew for sure that he never wanted to grow up. He was perfectly happy to be nearly thirteen forever. He'd have his hormones surgically removed if necessary.

129

Either that or he was going to have to somehow travel back in time at regular intervals and hope that no one noticed when at some point his little brothers were actually older than him.

"Grandpa?" said Norm uncertainly.

"What?" said Grandpa.

"Do you like going to IKEA?"

"IKEA?" said Grandpa.

Norm nodded.

"Absolutely love it," said Grandpa. "Can't get enough of the place."

That was it then, thought Norm. If Grandpa liked IKEA then there really was no hope. He was doomed. It really was all downhill from here.

"Had you going there, didn't I?" said Grandpa, his eyes crinkling in the corners.

Norm breathed a massive sigh of relief. But before he could say anything else there was a sudden noise downstairs.

KERASSHHH!!!

A noise that sounded to Norm suspiciously like the sound of breaking glass.

CHAPTER 12

Norm appeared in the doorway to find Brian lying on the floor – and a red-faced Dave sitting on top of him. It was an unlikely scenario, Dave being both younger **and** smaller than Brian – but also, Norm had to admit, a pretty flipping funny one too.

"Get him off me!" yelled Brian.

Norm laughed.

"I'm not joking, Norman!" said Brian. "Get him off me!"

It was only then that Norm noticed
the smashed picture frame
on the floor. The one
which until very recently
had contained the old
black-and-white photo of
Grandpa looking like one
of The Beatles.

"Who did that?"

"He did!" said Dave, pointing to Brian.

"No, **he** did!" said Brian, pointing to Dave.

"I'm telling!" said Dave.

"No, **I'm** telling!" said Brian.

Personally, Norm couldn't have cared less who
did it, or who was going to tell. All Norm knew was
that knowing his flipping luck, **he'd** get the blame

despite not even being in the room at the time! Frankly, he could've been in an entirely different continent and he'd **still** end up getting the blame. He always flipping did.

"What were you doing with it in the first place?" said Norm.

Brian and Dave looked at each other.

"Well?" said Norm.

"I'm worried about Grandpa, you know..." said Brian before trailing off.

"Shut up, Brian!" said Dave.

"Yeah, shut up, Brian," said Norm.

"What's going on?" said Grandpa, appearing in the doorway next to Norm.

"Nothing, Grandpa," said Dave, getting off Brian. "We're just playing."

"Oh, I see," said Grandpa, noticing the picture frame.

"It was an accident, Grandpa! Honest!" said Brian, standing up.

Grandpa shrugged. He didn't seem even remotely bothered. "Doesn't matter."

"Really?" said Brian.

"Course not," said Grandpa. "It's only a picture frame."

Brian breathed a huge sigh of relief.

"Yeah, Brian," said Norm. "It's not like someone's died."

The room fell suddenly silent. Never mind being quiet enough to hear a pin drop, thought Norm. It was quiet enough to hear a pin drop in the next flipping street!

"No offence, Grandpa," said Dave.

"What do you mean, no offence?" said Grandpa.

"Brian thinks…"

"What?" said Grandpa.

"That you're going to, you know…"

"I'm going to **what?**"

"Die!" wailed Brian.

Grandpa frowned, his cloud-like eyebrows momentarily moving just a little bit closer together than normal. "Well, I **am**."

Brian looked horrified. "What?"

"We all are," said Grandpa.

Brian looked even more horrified. "What?"

"We're all going to die," said Grandpa. "Eventually."

That did it. Brian burst into floods of tears and flung himself at Grandpa. Grandpa wasn't a big fan of hugging, but dutifully put his arms round his grandson nevertheless.

"We're born. We die," said Grandpa. "That's what happens."

We change, we stink, thought Norm. Didn't mean you had to talk about it though.

But Grandpa hadn't finished. "Look at you boys. You're growing. I'm shrinking."

It was true. Grandpa was shrinking. Well, according to the felt-tip marks on the kitchen wall he was, anyway. The ones with names and dates next to them, to show how tall everyone was. Grandpa's marks were the only marks actually getting lower.

Grandpa 2009
Grandpa 2010
Grandpa 2011
Grandpa 2012
Norm 2012
Brian 2012
Norm 2011
Brian 2011
Dave 2011
Brian 2010

"It's the circle of life," said Grandpa.

"That reminds me, Grandpa," said Dave. "Can I take you into school please?"

"What for?" said Grandpa, suspiciously.

"Show and tell," said Dave.

"Show and tell?" said Grandpa.

"Yeah," said Dave. "We've got to take in something old that doesn't work."

Grandpa's eyes crinkled slightly in the corners. "Cheeky monkey. Now let's get you little ones to bed, shall we?"

"'Kay, Grandpa," sniffled Brian.

"Have you eaten lots of sweets?" said Grandpa.

"Yes, Grandpa!" sang Brian and Dave together.

"Have you drunk lots of fizzy drinks?"

"Yes, Grandpa!" sang Brian and Dave again.

"Excellent," said Grandpa. "Night night then."

Brian looked puzzled. "Don't we have to clean our teeth first, Grandpa?"

"I wouldn't bother if I were you," said Grandpa. "The world might end tomorrow."

Brian and Dave looked at Grandpa expectantly, but Grandpa remained expressionless.

"What?" he said. "I'm not saying it's **going** to end. I said it **might** end."

Norm chuckled quietly to himself. If all this talk of death and the destruction of the planet hadn't made his little brothers sleepy, nothing would.

"Go on," said Grandpa.
"Off you go."

"Night, Grandpa," said Dave.

"Night, Grandpa," said Brian, still sniffling.

"Sweet dreams," grinned Norm.

CHAPTER 13

With Brian and Dave safely tucked up in bed, Grandpa and Norm settled down to watch television. Or at least Norm did. Grandpa seemed much more interested in continually zapping channels with the remote. Norm couldn't believe it. He thought it was supposed to be **kids** who couldn't concentrate on one thing for more than two seconds, not adults.

Grandpa appeared to have the attention span of a goldfish. Not only that but a goldfish with a particularly low boredom threshold.

"When I was your age there were no such things as remote controls," said Grandpa.

Norm pulled a face. He had no idea there were such things as **televisions** when Grandpa was his age, never mind flipping remotes.

"Mind you, there were only two channels in those days," said Grandpa.

"What?" said Norm. "You're kidding me, Grandpa! Only **two** channels?"

"Hard to imagine now, eh, Norman?"

Norm tried to imagine it.

Grandpa was right. It **was** hard.

"What happened if there was nothing decent on the other side?"

Grandpa shrugged. "You switched off."

"What?" said Norm.

"You switched the TV off and did something else instead."

"But..." said Norm.

"But what?" said Grandpa.

"How could you switch the TV off if there was no such thing as a remote?"

Grandpa looked at Norm. "Seriously?"

"Seriously," said Norm.

"We used to actually have to get up and **walk** to the television and switch it off by hand," said Grandpa.

"Whoa," said Norm.

"I know," said Grandpa. "Hard to believe, isn't it?"

Grandpa was wrong, thought Norm. It wasn't just **hard** to believe. It was **impossible** to believe. Switching off a telly by **hand?** No doubt his dad would approve of that. There'd be no chance of leaving a TV on standby overnight if there was no remote. Mind you, thought Norm, think of all the energy used walking backwards and forwards from the sofa. And not only that – think of all the carpet being worn out. If greenhouses and icebergs had something to do with global warming, figured Norm, there was every chance carpet did too.

"Look at all these channels," said Grandpa, zapping so fast his thumb was virtually a blur. "And nothing decent on any of them."

"What was it like, Grandpa?"

"What was **what** like?" said Grandpa.

"The olden days."

Grandpa turned to Norm, his eyes crinkling ever so slightly in the corners.

"The olden days?"

"Yeah," said Norm.

"Honestly?"

Norm nodded.

"Not all they're cracked up to be," said Grandpa.

"Really?" said Norm.

"Really," said Grandpa.

"How come?" said Norm.

"I'll tell you when you get back," said Grandpa.

"Where from?"

"The kitchen."

Norm pulled a face. "But I'm not going to the kitchen."

"You are now."

"What for?" said Norm.

"To switch the kettle on," said Grandpa. "Unless there's a remote for that as well?"

Norm laughed, but did as he was told anyway. By the time he reappeared less than a minute later, Grandpa had finally stopped zapping channels and was watching a programme about dolphins.

"What's up, Grandpa?" asked Norm. "You worn the battery out?"

Grandpa didn't reply. Dolphins were clearly more fascinating than Norm had previously thought. Not that Norm had thought much about dolphins previously.

"Want me to change channels, Grandpa?" grinned Norm. "I could do with the exercise."

But again there was no reply. Dolphins weren't **that** fascinating, were they? thought Norm.

"Grandpa?"

It was then that Norm noticed Grandpa's eyes were closed. Surely he couldn't have fallen asleep in that short space of time, could he? Hang on, thought Norm, his imagination suddenly whirring into overdrive. If Grandpa wasn't asleep, that must mean...

"Grandpa?" said Norm, immediately flying into a panic. "Wake up!
Oh my..."

"BOO!" yelled
Grandpa,
opening his
eyes and
sticking his
arms in
the air.

"*Aaaaaaaaargh!!!*"

screamed Norm.

"That's NOT flipping funny!"

"I think you'll find it is," said Grandpa, his eyes crinkling in the corners. "And mind your language."

Mind his language? thought Norm. Surely if ever there was an excuse for a bit of language it was thinking your grandpa had just kicked the flipping bucket.

From the hallway came the sound of the front door being opened. Looking around, Norm suddenly realised that the bits of broken picture frame still hadn't been tidied up. His brothers clearly weren't going to do it. Neither was Grandpa by the looks of things.

With a weary sigh of resignation, Norm began picking up the pieces of glass himself. He knew exactly what was going to happen next. And he was right. It did.

"Oh, no," said Norm's mum, walking into the room. "How could you, love?"

Norm shrugged. There was no point trying to explain. There never was.

"It's only a frame," said Grandpa.

"True," said Norm's mum, nodding. "It's a good excuse to go back to IKEA, I suppose."

Norm couldn't help smiling. Since when had his mum ever needed an excuse to go to IKEA?

"What, love?" said Norm's mum.

"Nothing, Mum."

"NORMAN?"

yelled Norm's dad from the kitchen.

Gordon flipping Bennet, thought Norm. What was he going to get the blame for now? The price of fishfingers? A worldwide cheese shortage? The break of flipping dawn?

"How many times have I told you about not overfilling the kettle?" said Norm's dad appearing in the doorway, the vein on the side of his head beginning to throb. Not that Norm noticed.

Norm thought for a moment. "Once?"

"And don't answer back!"

"But…"

"No buts, Norman!" said Norm's dad. "Enough is enough!"

"Go to bed, love, there's a good boy," said Norm's mum. "We'll talk about this in the morning."

"We will **not** talk about this in the morning!" snapped Norm's dad. "I warned him!"

Norm's mum looked concerned. "What are you going to do?"

"I'll think of something!"

"Yeah, right," muttered Norm under his breath.

"What?" said Norm's dad.

"Nothing," said Norm.

"And don't answer back!"

CHAPTER 14

"So?" said Mikey.

"So what?" said Norm.

"Did she say anything else?"

"Did **who** say anything else?"

"Chelsea."

Gordon flipping Bennet, thought Norm, skidding to a halt and putting his feet on the ground. It was as if he and Mikey were having two entirely different conversations. "When? What are you on about, Mikey?"

"When she said to say hi to me," said Mikey, jamming on his brakes and very nearly crashing into the back of Norm. "You were about to tell me?"

"I was?" said Norm.

"On Facebook?"

"What?"

Norm was still feeling slightly groggy and half asleep. He'd been in the middle of a dream about having his tonsils removed by a giant squid when he'd woken to find John slobbering all over his face again. It hadn't been the best start to a Sunday morning.

"Last night?" said Mikey.

"Oh right!" said Norm, finally remembering that he'd left Mikey dangling mid-chat when Grandpa had turned up unannounced the previous evening. "Why didn't you just say that in the first flipping place, Mikey, you doughnut?"

Mikey hesitated. "Dunno. It's a bit…"

"A bit what?" said Norm.

"Difficult," said Mikey.

"What is? Talking and biking at the same time?"

"No," said Mikey. "It's just a bit…"

"What?" said Norm, starting to get annoyed.

"Awkward," mumbled Mikey.

Norm pulled a face. "So why flipping ask then?"

Mikey shrugged. "Dunno."

"Yeah, well, neither do I," said Norm, setting off again. "You coming, or what?"

Mikey started pedalling after Norm. It didn't take long to catch up. Despite the fact that it was **Norm** who was the one who was mad keen on bikes and biking – and **Norm** who'd pimped his bike up – it was actually **Mikey** who was the slightly better rider. Mikey knew it. Norm knew it. Mikey knew that Norm knew it. Norm knew that Mikey knew that Norm knew it. It was **SO** flipping unfair, thought Norm.

They rode on in silence for a few minutes – Norm keen to perfect his mountain-biking skills, Mikey perfectly happy to tag along for the ride. It wasn't exactly the most challenging of terrains, but in the absence of any actual mountains the woods at the back of the shopping precinct would just have to do.

"So?" said Mikey eventually.

"So what?" said Norm.

"**Did** she say anything else?"

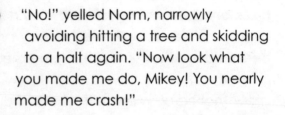

"No!" yelled Norm, narrowly avoiding hitting a tree and skidding to a halt again. "Now look what you made me do, Mikey! You nearly made me crash!"

"Sorry, Norm," said Mikey, also skidding to a halt – and far too nice to say what they both knew. That Norm nearly crashing had had absolutely nothing to do with him.

"What's the big deal, anyway? Why are you so bothered if she said anything else, or not?"

Mikey shrugged. "Just wondered."

"She's *so* flipping annoying," said Norm.

Mikey didn't reply. He seemed slightly distracted.

"Isn't she?" said Norm.

"What?" said Mikey.

"Chelsea," said Norm. "She's so flipping annoying."

"Oh yeah, she's well annoying. Definitely, yeah."

Norm looked at Mikey and smiled.

"What?" said Mikey.

"You don't..."

Mikey didn't even let Norm finish the sentence. "Course I don't. Don't be ridiculous."

"But..."

"Don't even go there, Norm."

"All right, all right," said Norm. "Calm down. Keep your hair on! I was just wondering, that's all."

"Yeah, well, don't," said Mikey.

They set off again. Again Norm took the lead. Again Mikey was perfectly happy to follow.

"Sorry, Norm," said Mikey after a while.

"What for?" said Norm.

"For snapping."

"That's OK."

"Must be my hormones," said Mikey.

The mere mention of Mikey's hormones was enough to make Norm feel slightly sick. He knew he needed to change the subject and fast. If he didn't he was in danger of losing his lunch. Well, losing his breakfast anyway. Norm hadn't actually had lunch yet.

"Do you ever get random friend requests on

Facebook, Mikey?"

"No such thing," said Mikey.

"As what?" said Norm.

"A random friend request."

"What do you mean?"

"There'll be a connection somewhere."

"Really?" said Norm.

"Definitely," said Mikey. "I got a friend request from some guy I didn't know."

"And?" said Norm expectantly.

"Turned out he was a friend of a friend of a friend."

"Who?" said Norm.

"Who what?"

"Who was the friend?"

"The friend the friend was a friend of?"

"Yeah," said Norm.

"You," said Mikey.

"Seriously?"

"Seriously."

"Whoa," said Norm.

By now they'd reached the steps at the back of the precinct and had skidded to a halt.

"Did you get one, then?" said Mikey.

"Get what?" said Norm.

"A friend request."

"Oh right," said Norm. "Yeah, I did, actually."

"Who from?"

What was that name again? thought Norm,

scratching his head. Not that it had much effect. He was wearing his helmet. "Ryan O'Toole?"

It was only after Norm had said it aloud that he suddenly realised. Rhino Tool! So it **wasn't** just an animal followed by the first word Brian could think of after all. It was a proper name. Ryan O'Toole. He actually existed!

"Nah, don't know him," said Mikey. "But there'll be a connection somewhere, Norm. There always is."

"Yeah," said Norm. "I think I know what it might be."

"There you go," said Mikey. "Let's go and get a drink from the supermarket."

Norm would have liked nothing better than to have had a drink. There was just one problem. He didn't have any money on him.

"I'm not thirsty," said Norm.

Mikey looked at Norm. "Really?"

"Yeah, really!" said Norm.

Mikey had a pretty good idea that Norm wasn't being entirely truthful. He also had a pretty good idea **why** Norm wasn't being entirely truthful. But the last thing he wanted to do was embarrass his friend.

"I need some stuff anyway."

"Stuff?" said Norm. "What kind of stuff?"

Mikey hesitated slightly. "Just, you know..."

"What?" said Norm.

Mikey sighed. "If you must know, I need to get some more deodorant."

"Why?" said Norm.

"Why do you think? I stink!"

162

Norm pulled a face. "Why do I think you stink?"

Mikey sighed again. "Why do you think I need to get more deodorant? Because I stink, **that's** why!"

"Mikey?"

"Yeah?"

"We **both stink!**" said Norm. "We're all sweaty from biking!"

"But I stink even more," said Mikey.

Gordon flipping Bennet, thought Norm. When was Mikey going to stop going on about his flipping hormones? Unless of course it was his hormones that were making him go on about his flipping hormones? Whatever it was, he wished he'd stop.

"Come on then," said Norm, bumping down the steps. "I'll race you. Last one there's a girl!"

Mikey pulled a face. "I'm not sure you should say that, Norm."

But it was too late. Norm had already gone.

CHAPTER 15

"Sure you're not thirsty, Norm?" said Mikey, standing in front of the chilled drinks cabinet, basket in hand.

"What?" said Norm, still a bit miffed that the security guard hadn't actually allowed him to bring his bike into the supermarket, insisting instead that he should lock it up outside like everyone else.

"Sure you don't want a drink?"

"Nah, you're all right," said Norm, checking his phone for texts even though he already knew he hadn't got any. The only person likely to have texted was stood right next to him. But Norm also knew that he couldn't look directly at the drinks. Not without drooling all over the floor anyway.

"It's my treat," said Mikey.

What? thought Norm. Why hadn't Mikey said that in the first flipping place? What should he do now? He didn't want to make it **too** obvious that the only reason he'd suddenly changed his mind was because he wasn't going to have to pay. The problem now was how to say yes – and still keep his dignity reasonably intact.

"Final answer?" said Mikey, like a TV quiz show host.

Norm sighed. "Go on then. If it makes you happy, Mikey."

"Excellent, help yourself," said Mikey, plucking a can from a shelf and reading the label out loud. "'Rad Bull! The sugar-free energy drink with no additives or artificial flavourings!' Mmm. Sounds great, doesn't it, Norm?"

What was Mikey on about now? thought Norm. Not only did it *not* sound great, it sounded abso-flipping-lutely disgusting! Sugar-free? No additives or artificial flavourings? So basically just water, then? What was the point of that? But then, Norm wasn't a big fan of so-called "healthy" food. As far as Norm was concerned, pizza counted as one of his five-a-day – as long as all the

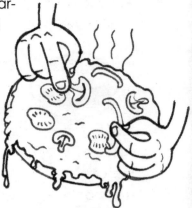

vegetables had been scraped off first. As for drinks? The more garishly coloured the better as far as Norm was concerned. In fact, never mind **no** additives or artificial flavourings. Norm couldn't get **enough** additives or artificial flavourings.

"Oh, look, it's buy one get one free, Norm!" said Mikey. "No pressure!"

"Nah, don't worry," said Norm, reaching for a luminous green drink which, according to the label, would have his pee glowing in the dark or his money back. Or at least, Mikey's money back anyway.

"Come on," said Mikey, heading down the aisle.

But Norm wasn't listening. He was too busy figuring out how to open the drink.

"Oi," said a voice.

Norm looked up to see the security guard eyeballing him.

"What do you think you're doing now?"

Norm pulled a face. What did it **look** like he was doing? "Opening my drink."

"I can see that."

So why flipping ask then? thought Norm.

"You've got to pay first."

"Pardon?" said Norm.

"You've got to pay for it first. **Then** you can open it."

"But I haven't actually opened it yet," said Norm.

"No, but you were about to," said the security guard.

True, thought Norm. He **had** been about to. And if this guy hadn't come along, he probably would have done by now.

"That's twice I've had to have words with you."

At least he could count, thought Norm. But honestly – what was the big deal? He'd **almost** opened a drink. *"So flipping what?"* Hadn't this guy got more important things to do? Like checking yoghurts to make sure they hadn't gone past their sell-by dates or something?

"Do it again and you're out."

Norm could hardly believe what he was hearing.

"What?"

"Next time you break a rule you're out," said the security guard.

"But I didn't break a rule," said Norm.

"But you **nearly** did," said the security guard.

Norm was no expert in legal matters, but he was reasonably certain that he couldn't be thrown out of a supermarket for **nearly** doing something. Frankly, even if he **had** opened his drink it wasn't exactly the most serious of offences in the great scheme of things. It wasn't like he'd farted next to the cheese counter. Not that anyone would be able to tell if he **had** farted next to the cheese counter. The smell was bad enough already without Norm adding to it.

Norm briefly thought about asking the security guard whether he had a list of other rules and regulations. Just so that he was clear what else he couldn't do. Or rather what else he couldn't **nearly** do. But he didn't. Life was too short, thought Norm. As well as being unbelievably unfair, obviously. And besides, he'd lost Mikey. Well – not actually **lost** Mikey. He was presumably still somewhere in the supermarket. But where?

Norm started wandering down the aisle.

"I'm watching you!" called the security guard.

Yeah, whatever, thought Norm,
rounding a corner to find
Mikey loading up his
basket with cans of Stynx.

"Flipping heck, Mikey! Is
there a special offer on?"

"What?" said Mikey.

"How many are you getting?"

"What's it got to do with
you, Norm?"

"I was only asking."

"Well, don't."

"'Kay."

Mikey seemed somewhat sheepish. "Sorry, Norm. I don't know what's wrong with me. It's my…"

"Hormones?" said Norm.

"Yeah," said Mikey. "They're making me act all…"

"Weird?" said Norm.

"Are you going to finish all my…"

"Sentences?" said Norm.

Norm smiled. But Mikey didn't react at all. He was clearly troubled by something. But what? wondered Norm. **What** was making his best friend act all weird? It couldn't have **only** been his hormones. There was obviously something else besides. For a second, Norm almost felt sorry for Mikey. He would have almost felt sorry for a bit longer if an all-too-familiar voice hadn't suddenly piped up.

"Hello, Mikey! Hello, **Norman!**"

Norm sighed. It was bad enough Chelsea making fun of his name over the garden fence, never mind in the middle of the flipping supermarket. But before Norm could say anything, Mikey had handed him the basket.

"Here you go, Norm!"

Norm pulled a face. "Eh? What?"

"I'm fed up carrying it for you!" said Mikey.

"But..."

"Carry it yourself!"

What on earth was Mikey going on about? wondered Norm, looking at his friend for some kind of sign or clue. Mikey had his back to Chelsea. She wasn't able to see the look of sheer desperation on his face. But Norm could. And that was enough. It was all he needed to know for now. What was that expression? A friend indeed was a friend in need? Something like that, anyway, thought Norm.

"Right," said Norm, taking the basket. "Thanks, Mikey. I owe you one."

"My, my, **Norman**," said Chelsea, eyeing the basket. "That **is** a lot of deodorant."

"Yeah," laughed Norm. "It is, isn't it?"

"For **one** person," said Chelsea.

"Not necessarily," said Mikey.

"Oh?" said Chelsea, raising an eyebrow.

"They might just be stocking up," said Mikey.

"*They?*" grinned Chelsea.

"**Norm,**" said Mikey.

"**Norm?**" said Chelsea.

"**Obviously,**" said Mikey.

Norm suddenly felt like he was umpiring a tennis match. But a tennis match with no balls. Or rackets. Just words. Not only that but it was pretty obvious by now that, for whatever reason, Mikey didn't want Chelsea to think that it was **his** deodorant. And for now, anyway, Norm was happy to go along with it. Well – not particularly **happy** to go along with it. He just couldn't think of a good enough reason **not** to go along with it.

"I do get through an awful lot," said Norm.

"Really?" said Chelsea. "I had no idea you were that smelly, **Norman!**"

"Oh, definitely, yeah," said Norm. "I'm well whiffy, me."

As if to prove the point, Norm took one of the cans from the basket, shook it, popped the lid off and sprayed himself generously from head to foot.

"Right, that's it!" said the security guard, appearing from nowhere. "I warned you!"

"But..." said Norm.

"No buts," said the security guard. "Out!"

"Hello, Peter," said Chelsea, smiling sweetly.

"Oh, hello Chelsea," said the security guard, perfectly pleasantly. "I didn't see you there."

Uh? thought Norm. They **knew** each other? How come?

"Peter's my friend Chloe's dad," said Chelsea, as if she could read Norm's mind. "Aren't you, Peter?"

The security guard nodded sheepishly. "Mr O'Toole when I'm on duty if you don't mind, Chelsea."

Mr **O'Toole**? thought Norm. "Do you have a son called Ryan?"

"Are you still here?" said Mr O'Toole, immediately officious again.

What kind of stupid question was **that**? thought Norm. Of course he was still there. This guy was in the wrong flipping job if he couldn't see **that**!

"You're banned, by the way."

 said Norm.

"You heard."

It was true. Norm **had** heard. It was so unfair. If he was going to get banned from anywhere, why couldn't he get banned from flipping IKEA?

"Banned?" said Chelsea. "That's a bit harsh, isn't it?"

"I warned him."

"I know," said Chelsea. "But even so..."

"Rules are rules, Chelsea."

Chelsea hesitated slightly before narrowing her eyes. "Seen my mum lately, Pe...I mean, Mr O'Toole?"

"Pardon?"

"You heard," said Chelsea.

All of a sudden Mr O'Toole seemed slightly ill at ease. Not that Norm noticed.

"Erm, no, I haven't, not lately, no."

"Just wondered," said Chelsea. "So, er...is my friend here still banned, then?"

Norm was gobsmacked. Had Chelsea *really* just referred to him as her *friend?* Flipping typical, thought Norm. The world had finally gone mad

178

and no one had bothered telling him!

"Erm, no, he's not, no," muttered the security guard.

"Didn't think so," said Chelsea breezily. "Come on, **Norman**. Better go and pay for all that deodorant of yours!"

"Haven't got any money," blurted Norm without thinking and realised straightaway that he'd made a big mistake. The question was, thought Norm, had Chelsea noticed?

"Really?" said Chelsea, raising not one but two eyebrows. "You **do** surprise me."

Oops, thought Norm. She'd noticed.

"It's OK, Norm," said Mikey quickly. "I'll lend you the money."

"What?" said Norm, by now becoming just a teensy bit confused.

"I'll lend you the money," said Mikey. "You can pay me back later."

"Oh, right," said Norm. "Thanks, Mikey."

"Looks like that's **another** one you owe Mikey, **Norman**."

"What do you mean?" said Norm.

"First he carries all that deodorant for you – now he's going to lend you some money!"

"So?" said Norm.

"Some guy," said Chelsea, fixing Mikey with a look before heading for the checkouts.

CHAPTER 16

"***Well?***" said Chelsea, once they were safely outside the supermarket.

"**Well, well,**" said Mikey.

"**Well, well, well,**" said Norm, wondering whether this was some kind of game. If so, it was a pretty rubbish one. It would never catch on.

"Have you got something to say to me?" said Chelsea.

This should be good, thought Norm, turning to Mikey expectantly. But Mikey didn't reply.

"I'm talking to you, ***Norman***," said Chelsea.

"What?" said Norm.

"Have you got something to say to me?"

Norm shrugged. "I dunno. Have I?"

"Seriously?" said Chelsea.

"Seriously," said Norm.

Chelsea laughed. "Unbelievable!"

"What is?" said Norm.

"I just stopped you getting banned in there!"

"Yeah, so?" said Norm. "I didn't ask you to."

"Well, I did, anyway."

Norm pulled a face. "What do you want? A medal?"

"No, I don't want a medal!" said Chelsea. "A simple **_thank you_** would be nice though!"

Norm sighed. "Thanks."

"It's too late now!" said Chelsea.

Gordon flipping Bennet, thought Norm. Did she want him to say thank you or not?

"It was really good of you," mumbled Mikey, staring at the ground.

"Thank you, Mikey," said Chelsea, smiling sweetly. "I'm glad someone's got manners."

"Creep," muttered Norm.

"What was that, **_Norman?_**"

"Nothing," said Norm. "What was all that stuff about your mum then?"

Chelsea grinned. "Chloe's dad fancies her."

"What?"
"Aw, that's gross!"

"Do you mind?" said Chelsea. "That's my mum you're talking about!"

"Yeah, I know, but..."

"But what?" said Chelsea.

Norm thought for a moment. "I dunno. It's just..."

"Just what?" said Chelsea.

Norm couldn't quite put his finger on what he found so gross about the idea of someone fancying someone else's mum. He wasn't even sure he **wanted** to put his finger on what he found so gross about someone fancying someone else's mum. He just knew that it was somehow gross, that was all.

"There's nothing wrong with it," said Chelsea. "My mum and dad don't live together. And neither do Chloe's mum and dad. They can do what they want. They're adults!"

Exactly, thought Norm. ***That*** was what was so gross! They were adults! Adults were supposed to go to IKEA with each other – not ***fancy*** each other. OK, so they still had hormones and stuff, but even so. There was something about it that was just ***wrong***.

"I think it's quite sweet actually," said Chelsea. "I quite like the idea of having a little baby brother or sister."

That's it, thought Norm. There was a line – and Chelsea had just crossed it. The thought of anyone over the age of twenty so much as holding hands was bad enough. The idea of them actually snogging – or anything else for that matter – was frankly unimaginable. Which was just as well really, as Norm didn't particularly want to imagine it anyway.

"Please stop," said Norm.

"What?" said Chelsea. "All I said was..."

"Seriously," said Norm.
"Please stop!
I'm begging you."

"But..." said Chelsea.

"Chelsea?"

"Yeah?"

"Shut up!"
yelled Norm.

Chelsea laughed.

"I really don't see what's so funny," said Norm.
"It's disgusting!"

"It's not disgusting," said Chelsea. "Is it, Mikey?"

"What?" said Mikey.

"Someone fancying someone else?" said Chelsea,
tilting her head and smiling. "That's not disgusting,
is it?"

"Erm...no, don't suppose so," mumbled Mikey, staring at the ground again and immediately going bright red. Not that Norm noticed.

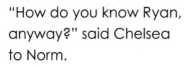

"How do you know Ryan, anyway?" said Chelsea to Norm.

"Who?" said Norm.

"Ryan O'Toole?" said Chelsea. "Chloe's little brother?"

So they **were** related, thought Norm. "I don't."

"Uh?" said Chelsea.

"I got a friend request from him on Facebook."

"Right," said Chelsea.

"See, Norm?" said Mikey. "I told you there'd be a connection somewhere. There always is."

"How old is he?" said Norm.

Chelsea thought for a moment. "Ryan? Not sure. Nine? Ten, maybe?"

So about Brian's age then, thought Norm. Maybe that was another connection?

"Oh well, gotta go, I suppose," said Chelsea. "What you up to later?"

Norm shrugged. "Nothing much."

Chelsea giggled. "I wasn't talking to **you**, Norman."

"What?" said Norm. "Oh, right."

Tee hee

It took a moment or two for Norm to fully realise what Chelsea had just said. Or rather, what Chelsea **hadn't** just said. She hadn't actually needed to say it. If she wasn't talking to Norm, then...

"**Well?**" said Chelsea.

　　　　　　　"**Well, well,**" said Mikey.

"**Well, well, well,**" said Norm.

CHAPTER 17

"Well?" said Norm.

"Don't **you** start, Norm!" said Mikey.

They were biking back through the woods – Norm in the lead as usual, Mikey tagging along behind as usual. The only difference was, Mikey wasn't finding it quite so easy tagging along behind, what with all the cans of Stynx currently clanking and rattling about in his backpack.

"I thought you said you didn't fancy her," said Norm.

"I didn't!" said Mikey.

Norm pulled a face. Did Mikey mean that he didn't **fancy** Chelsea – or that he hadn't actually **said** that? He hadn't even let Norm finish the question when Norm had tried to ask it earlier on. Mikey had almost bitten Norm's head off!

"I'm a bit confused," said Norm. "Do you fancy Chelsea, or not?"

"No!" yelled Mikey. "I do **not** fancy Chelsea! OK?"

"OK," said Norm.

"She fancies me!"

"Whoa!" said Norm, jamming on his brakes so violently that he very nearly went flying over the handlebars.

"Tell me about it!" said Mikey, doing the same.

"How do you know?" said Norm.

"Have you not noticed the way she's been looking at me lately?" said Mikey.

"No," said Norm.

It was true. Norm **hadn't** noticed the way Chelsea had been looking at Mikey lately. Then again, Norm wouldn't have noticed if it had been raining fish lately.

"And she keeps saying stuff too."

"What? You mean on Facebook?" said Norm.

Mikey nodded. "Yeah, obviously."

"What kind of stuff?"

"Just...you know."

"No, I don't," said Norm. "That's why I'm flipping asking, you doughnut! What kind of stuff?"

Mikey seemed to hesitate. "Can't remember."

Norm looked at Mikey. "Mikey?"

"What?"

"I think you can."

Mikey sighed. "She said..."

"What?"

"She said I had nice..."

"What?" said Norm, getting more and more exasperated.

"Ears," said Mikey.

"Pardon?" said Norm.

"She said I had nice ears," said Mikey.

Norm laughed. "You're kidding me, right?"

Mikey pulled a face. "No, why? What's wrong with my ears?"

"What?" said Norm. "Nothing's wrong with your ears, Mikey. They're perfectly nice ears. It's just..."

"What?"

"Dunno," said Norm. "What else has she said?"

Mikey thought for a moment. "She said she likes my..."

"Your what?" said Norm.

"My bottom...."

"What!" yelled Norm.

"My bottom lip," said Mikey.

Norm started to smile. "You're winding me up aren't you, Mikey?"

"I'm not, Norm! Honest!"

This conversation, decided Norm, was getting weirder by the second. Chelsea liked Mikey's ears? And his bottom lip? Just the bottom one? What was wrong with his top lip?

"Is that it?" said Norm.

Mikey seemed to hesitate again. "No. She wrote a..."

"A what?" said Norm.

"Gordon flipping Bennet, Mikey! Get on with it!"

"A poem," mumbled Mikey.

"A poem?"

Mikey nodded.

"Whoa," said Norm.

"Tell me about it," said Mikey.

"No, Mikey," said Norm. "You tell *me* about it."

"Uh?"

"Tell me what the poem was."

Mikey looked horrified. "No way!"

"Go on!" pleaded Norm.

"Seriously, Norm. There's no way!"

Norm thought for a moment. He wouldn't normally give two hoots to hear some stupid poem. In fact never mind *two* hoots. He wouldn't normally give any hoots at all. But this was different somehow. This was serious.

"I'll pay you."

"What?" said Mikey.

"I'll pay you," said Norm. "If you tell me the poem."

Mikey laughed.

"Seriously, Mikey. I'll pay you. I mean, I don't actually have any money on me at the moment. But I'll owe you."

Mikey stroked his chin. "How much?"

Good question, thought Norm. How much was a poem actually worth? He'd still got the £10 his dad had given him for going for a walk with Dave. Less the £2 he said he'd give to Dave.

"A pound," said Norm.

"Two pounds," said Mikey.

"One-fifty."

"'Kay," said Mikey. "One-fifty."

The pair shook hands to seal the deal.

"Come on then," said Norm. "Let's hear it."

"'Kay," said Mikey. "Here goes."

Norm waited whilst Mikey cleared his throat before looking around to make sure no one else was watching or listening.

"Oh, Mikey, oh, Mikey," began Mikey.

So far, so good, thought Norm.

"I love it when you ride your bikey."

Mikey stopped. "There."

Norm pulled a face. "Is that it?"

Mikey nodded.

"'Oh, Mikey, oh, Mikey, I love it when you ride your bikey'?"

Mikey nodded again. Clearly the experience of recounting the poem had been an emotionally draining one.

"That's rubbish!" laughed Norm.

"What?" said Mikey.

"It's rubbish!" said Norm.

Mikey looked unsure. "Do you think so?"

"I don't **think** so!" said Norm. "I flipping **know** so! Honestly, Mikey! Even I could write a better poem than that! And I'm pants at poems!"

Mikey didn't say anything. He seemed lost in

thought. Subdued almost.

"Sorry, Mikey," said Norm. "I didn't mean to upset you."

"It's OK, I'm not bothered," said Mikey. "You're right. It's hardly Shakespeare, is it?"

"Who?" said Norm.

"Doesn't matter," said Mikey, looking at his watch. "Come on. We'd better get going."

Mikey waited for Norm to set off again. But Norm showed no sign of going anywhere.

"What's up?" said Mikey.

"Nothing," grinned Norm. "Just trying to think what rhymes with 'Chelsea'..."

CHAPTER 18

Norm got home on the stroke of lunchtime.

"Have you washed your hands, love?" said Norm's mum as Norm sat down at the table.

"Yeah," said Norm.

Norm's dad fixed Norm with a withering look.

"What?" said Norm innocently. "I have."

"Your mother means have you washed your hands since you got back, Norman? Not have you **ever** washed your hands."

"I'm saving water, Dad," said Norm. "I only wash when necessary."

"Well, it's necessary now," said Norm's dad. "So do as you're told."

Brian sniggered.

"Shut your face, Brian,"

said Norm, getting up again and heading for the stairs.

"And no going on the computer!" Norm's dad called after him.

Norm sighed. Why did his dad have to go and say that? He had had no intention of going on the computer. The thought had never even crossed his mind. Till now! Now it was all he could think of. Now it was going to take enormous willpower **not** to go on the computer. And if there was one thing Norm didn't have, it was enormous willpower. What little bit of willpower Norm **did** have had the breaking strain of a Kit Kat.

That was Norm's excuse anyway, as he sat down in front of the computer and logged on. The first thing he noticed was that he hadn't done anything about Ryan O'Toole's friend request. The second thing he noticed was that he'd received a message from Mikey, pleading with him not to say anything to anyone about the poem from Chelsea.

If there was a third thing, Norm didn't get the chance to notice it because of a sudden shout from the hallway.

"Norman!"

Norm said nothing. He knew that if he did it would be a dead giveaway. His dad would know instantly where he was and what he was up to. If only he could throw his voice. What an incredibly useful superpower *that* would be!

"You're not on the computer, are you?" yelled Norm's dad, instantly suspicious.

Again Norm chose to say nothing. Besides, he was far too busy tiptoeing as quietly as possible along the landing. The only trouble was, Norm was so focused on tiptoeing quietly that he completely forgot about the tell-tale creaky floorboard.

"What was that?" said Norm's dad.

"What was what, Dad?" said Norm, appearing as if by magic at the top of the stairs.

"That creaking sound?"

"Creaking sound?" said Norm. "I didn't hear any creaking sound, Dad. Must've been my stomach rumbling!"

Norm's dad looked at Norm, the vein on the side of his head beginning to throb. "That was some rumble."

"Yeah, well, I'm really hungry, Dad," said Norm, running down the stairs.

"Were you on the computer just now, Norman?"

"No, Dad."

"Because if you were, I'll...I'll..."

What will you do? thought Norm. Nothing, probably. Same as usual.

"I don't know what I'll do," said Norm's dad as Norm passed him. "But I'll do something!"

Sure you will, thought Norm, sitting down at the table again. "What's for lunch, Mum?"

"Pulses marinated in tomato sauce, served on a bed of lightly scorched bread," said Norm's mum.

Norm pulled a face. "Uh?"

"Beans on toast," said Norm's mum, plonking a plate in front of him.

Brian sniggered.

"Shut your face, Brian!" said Norm. "That's twice I've told you now!"

"Today, you mean?" said Brian.

Norm sighed. "Yes, today."

"Yesterday?" said Brian.

Gordon flipping Bennet, thought Norm. Was Brian **deliberately** trying to wind him up? Because if he was, it was abso-flipping-lutely working. "Do you know Ryan O'Toole, by the way?"

"Ryan O'Toole?" said Brian.

"That's who…" began Dave, before immediately stopping again.

Norm looked at Dave. "That's who what?"

"Nothing," said Dave, quickly.

Norm continued to look at his youngest brother. Whatever he'd been about to say, he'd suddenly decided not to say it. But why?

"What?" said Dave, irritably. "I was thinking of someone else."

Norm raised his right eyebrow. "Who?"

Dave thought for a moment. "Ryan O'Riley."

Norm raised his left eyebrow to keep the other one company. "Oh, really?"

"No," said Dave. "O'Riley."

"Hmm," said Norm. He had a feeling that Dave knew **precisely** who Ryan O'Toole was. More importantly perhaps, he had a feeling he knew precisely **why** Dave was acting so cagily all of a sudden.

"He's in my year at school," said Brian.

"Who is?" said Norm. "Ryan O'Toole?"

Brian nodded.

"Right," said Norm. "That would explain it."

"Explain what?" said Dave, sounding slightly panicky.

"Why I've got a friend request from him on Facebook," said Norm.

"Oh, right," said Dave.

Norm looked at Dave.

"What?" said Dave. "Why do you keep looking at me like that, Norman?"

Norm shrugged. "No reason."

"So?" said Norm's dad from the doorway.

Nobody else said anything. Norm looked up to find everyone staring at him. Including his dad.

"What?" said Norm.

"Anything you'd like to say to me, Norman?"

Norm thought for a moment. There were so many things he would like to say to his dad. How long had he got?

"I thought you told me you hadn't been on the computer?"

Ah, thought Norm. So **that** was why his dad was staring at him.

"It was **still** on," said Norm's dad. "Wasting energy and money as usual!"

Oops, thought Norm.

"And don't even **think** about blaming your brothers," said Norm's dad. "They were down here the whole time."

"'Kay, Dad," said Norm. "Sorry, Dad."

"So you're admitting it then? You **were** on the computer?"

Norm nodded.

"Right," said Norm's dad.

Right, what? thought Norm. What was his dad going to do about it?

Abso-Flipping-lutely zilch,

that's what!

"I know what you're thinking, Norman."

"What, Dad?"

"You're thinking, so what?
You're thinking, he's all talk.
You're thinking, he's not
actually going to do anything
about it."

Whoa, thought Norm.
That was pretty
flipping freaky.

"Am I right, Norman?"

"Erm..." said Norm.

"I'll take that as a yes then,"
said Norm's dad.

"What *are* you going to do about it, Dad?"
said Brian.

"Shut up, Brian!" hissed Norm. "If I have to tell you
one more time!"

"That'll be three times," said Brian.

Norm and Dave looked at each other for a moment. Dave had gone very quiet. And Norm thought he knew why. Not only that, but Dave knew that Norm thought he knew why. There was obviously more to this whole Ryan O'Toole thing than met the eye. But what? thought Norm. It was time to find out.

"Fancy taking John for a walk after lunch, Dave?" said Norm.

"OK," said Dave.

Norm's mum smiled. "That's very nice of you, love."

"Can I come too?" said Brian.

Norm sighed. "Only if you promise to shut up."

"Excellent," said Norm's dad. "Your mum and I need to talk."

"We do?" said Norm's mum.

"We do," said Norm's dad, turning to Norm and half smiling.

CHAPTER 19

"Let's cut straight to the chase," said Norm the second they set foot outside the house.

"What chase?" said Brian. "I thought we were going for a walk?"

"And I thought I told you to shut up, Brian."

"You did," said Brian.

"So why haven't you?"

"Why haven't I what?" said Brian.

"Shut up," said Norm, already regretting the decision to let his middle brother tag along. And they hadn't even reached the bottom of the drive yet.

"Yeah, shut up, Brian," said Dave. "It's all your fault anyway."

"What is?" said Brian.

Dave glared venomously at Brian.
"You know!"

"Do I?" said Brian. "What are you on about, Dave?"

"You **know** what I'm on about, Brian!"

"No I don't," said Brian.

"Are you going to tell us or what, Dave?" said Norm.

Dave appeared to hesitate. "It's Ryan O'Toole. He's the one."

Norm nodded. He knew it was. He just needed to hear Dave say it. "You mean the one who's..."

"Bullying me. Yeah," said Dave.

Brian seemed genuinely surprised. "What?"

"You heard," said Dave.

"But..." said Brian.

"You and your *Lord of the Rings* cards!"

"What?" said Brian.

"What?" said Norm.

"He was supposed to be swapping some stupid card with Ryan O'Toole," said Dave. "Weren't you, Brian?"

Brian looked a bit sheepish. "Yeah, well, I changed my mind, didn't I? And it **wasn't** just any old stupid card actually, Dave! It was Gollum! So there!"

"Geek," muttered Dave.

"There's nothing geekish about **Lord of the Rings!**" said Brian, defensively. "And there's nothing geekish about collecting cards either. It's perfectly natural!"

"Yeah," said Dave, "if you're a geek!"

"I am **not** a geek!" said Brian.

"Yeah, whatever," said Dave, eyes blazing. "A deal's a deal, Brian!"

Norm pulled a face. He was struggling to make the connection between Brian not swapping a card with Ryan O'Toole – and Ryan O'Toole demanding a can of Stynx from Dave. "Can we fast-forward a bit?"

Dave looked at Norm. "It's hardly rocket science."

What isn't? thought Norm. What was Dave talking about flipping rockets for all of a sudden? Had he missed something? Never mind fast-flipping-forwarding, Norm needed to rewind!

"Ryan O'Toole's a chicken!" said Dave.

What? thought Norm. Ryan O'Toole was a **chicken?** He **definitely** needed to rewind. Preferably back to the beginning.

"He was miffed with **Brian**, but took it out on *me* instead! The little brother! The easy target!"

"Oh, right," said Norm. "I get it."

"No, Norman!" said Dave. "**You** don't get it! **I** get it!"

Norm and Brian both turned to Dave. By now Dave's chin had begun to wobble and his eyes had gone all watery.

"What?" said Dave. "Don't look at me like that!"

"What do you want me to do about it?" said Norm.

"I don't want you to do **anything** about it!" sniffed Dave.

Sniff
Sniff

"Really?" said Norm.

"Really," said Dave defiantly. "It's no big deal!"

That's OK, then, thought Norm, who had no great desire to do anything about it anyway. He'd kind of assumed that Dave would want him to at least have a word with Ryan O'Toole. Tell him to back off or whatever. But if Dave preferred to deal with things himself, that was abso-flipping-lutely fine by Norm. No point sticking his nose where it wasn't wanted. Which reminded Norm...

"Why deodorant, Dave?"

"What?" said Dave.

"Why does Ryan O'Toole want a can of Stynx?"

Dave shrugged. "Dunno. Don't care."

"It's a big thing at school," said Brian.

"What is?" said Norm.

"Stynx," said Brian.

"Really?" said Norm.

"Yeah," said Brian. "All these kids trying to be older than they really are. You can smell them a mile off. It's horrible!"

Brian was right, there, thought Norm. It **was** pretty horrible. Why would anyone want to be older than they actually were? What was wrong with being whatever age you happened to be at the time? Surely you'd got the rest of your life to get old?

"I'm really sorry, Dave," said Brian.

Dave looked at Brian for a moment. "Geek."

Brian put his hands in the air. "Guilty as charged."

And they all lived happily ever after, thought Norm. But even as he thought it, Norm had a funny feeling there was something they'd forgotten. But what?

"Weren't we supposed to be taking John for a walk?" said Brian.

That was it, thought Norm. The dog. He **knew** they'd forgotten something!

CHAPTER 20

Grandpa was sat in the kitchen when Norm walked in.

"'Ello, 'ello," he said. "And how's my least favourite grandson, today?"

"I don't know, Grandpa," said Norm, "but when I see Brian I'll ask him."

'ELLo, 'ello

Grandpa's eyes crinkled ever so slightly in the corners. "Very good, Norman. Very good."

"What?" said Norm, pulling a face. "I wasn't joking."

"Grandpa's just popped in to say goodbye, love," said Norm's mum.

Norm felt like he'd just run slap-bang into a brick wall. Had he heard his mum right? Grandpa was here to say **goodbye?**

"Not forever, you numpty," said Grandpa, who had the uncanny knack of being able to read Norm's mind. "Just for a couple of days."

Norm breathed a huge sigh of relief. "Oh, right! I thought you meant..."

"What? That I was about to kick the bucket?" said Grandpa.

Norm's mum looked shocked. "Dad!"

Grandpa shrugged. "What? It happens!"

"Yes, we know that, thank you very much," said Norm's mum.

Norm looked at Grandpa. "So **that's** why you can't babysit tonight then."

Grandpa's eyes crinkled a bit in the corners again. "You're not as daft as you look, Norman. No offence."

Norm smiled. "None taken."

"About that," said Norm's dad.

About what? thought Norm.

"Your dad's had an idea who might be able to babysit instead," said Norm's mum.

"Have you, Dad?" said Norm.

Norm's dad curled his lip. Either he was doing a really bad Elvis impression, thought Norm, or he was about to reveal some kind of evil master plan.

"Who?" said Norm.

Norm's dad chuckled. "Wouldn't you like to know?"

Yes! thought Norm. He flipping **would** like to know! Why did his dad think he was flipping asking?

"Becky," said Norm's mum, seemingly just as impatient as Norm was for Norm's dad to hurry up and spit it out.

Norm's face was an absolute picture. Unfortunately, it was a picture drawn by a two-year-old in crayon. Becky? His cousin Becky? "What?"

"Why not?" said Norm's mum. "She's sensible. She's reliable. She's perfect!"

Oh, she's perfect all right, thought Norm. **Too** flipping perfect! Just like her perfect flipping brothers! Always saving the world! Always best at this! Always captain of that! Always swimming with dolphins or dancing with penguins or whatever. Who flipping cared?

"This is a wind-up, right?" said Norm. "Please tell me you're not serious?"

"Still think I'm all talk, Norman?" said Norm's dad.

"What?" said Norm.

Norm's dad curled his lip again. "Next time you might think twice before overfilling the kettle. Or leaving the TV on standby overnight. Or going on the computer when I've told you not to."

"Oh, right," said Norm. So this really **was** some kind of evil master plan then? For once in his life, his dad had **threatened** to do something – and now it looked like he *was* actually going to do something! And credit where credit was due – this was just about the worst possible punishment Norm could think of. This was going to be like every nightmare he'd ever had, rolled into one. Frankly, he'd sooner have been banned from the Xbox for the next ten years than been babysat by Becky.

"What if..." began Norm.

"Norman?" said Norm's dad, holding a hand up and cutting Norm off mid-sentence.

"Yeah?" said Norm.

"This is strictly non-negotiable."

"What?" said Norm.

"It's happening, whether you like it or not," said Norm's dad. "End of."

Norm sighed.

"She's not that bad, is she?" said Grandpa.

Norm turned to Grandpa. "Not *that* bad, Grandpa? She's *worse!*"

"Now, now, love," said Norm's mum. "That's your cousin you're talking about."

"Yeah? So?" said Norm. "Doesn't mean I have to flipping like her!"

"Language!" said Norm's dad.

"'Snot fair," muttered Norm.

"Cheer up," said Grandpa.
"It's not the end of the world."

Maybe not, thought Norm.
But it wasn't far off.

"Well, I'll be off then," said Grandpa, getting to his feet and heading for the door.

Norm watched him go, concern etched across his face as he thought about what lay in store later on that day.

"Bye, Dad," said Norm's mum. "Have a lovely time!"

"I will," said Grandpa.

"Wait a minute, Grandpa!" said Norm, following Grandpa out of the room and catching up with him just as he was closing the front door.

"Do you really have to go?" said Norm.

"What?" said Grandpa gruffly. "Course I've got to go. I'll be late if I don't."

"No, I meant..."

"What?"

"Do you really **have** to go away for a few days?"

"Oh, I see," said Grandpa. "As a matter of fact, yes, I do."

"Why?" said Norm. "Where are you going?"

"Away," said Grandpa.

Obviously, thought Norm. "Where to?"

"**Away!**" said Grandpa, slowly and deliberately as if he was talking to a nearly-three-year-old and not a nearly-thirteen-year-old.

Norm thought for a moment. "Are you going *with* someone, Grandpa?"

Grandpa sighed. "Yes, Norman. If you must know, I

am going with someone."

"Who?" said Norm.

"A friend," said Grandpa.

"You mean..."

"A **lady** friend. Yes, Norman."

Whoa, thought Norm, wishing he hadn't asked.

"What's the problem?" said Grandpa, his eyes crinkling in the corners. "I told you I'd still got one or two hormones knocking about."

This was *way* too much information as far as Norm was concerned. He needed to think about something else, and quickly. **Anything** else! It didn't matter what.

And then it suddenly hit Norm. It was like being slapped in the face with a rubber chicken. Not that Norm had ever actually *been* slapped in the face with a rubber chicken before. Or any **other** kind of chicken for that matter. What he **really** needed to be thinking about right now was how to prevent what could possibly turn out to be the worst night of his life so far from happening. Was it too late to do anything about his perfect cousin Becky babysitting? Could she somehow be persuaded not to come? There just **had** to be a way, thought Norm. If only he could make contact with her. Not directly. That would be a bit too obvious. He'd be rumbled straight away and then who knows what might happen? No, he'd need to be a bit more subtle than that. A bit more devious. A bit more cunning.

"Facebook!"
blurted Norm all
of a sudden.

"Pardon?"
said Grandpa.

"Er, nothing,
Grandpa,"
said Norm.
"Just thinking out loud, that's all."

"Right, well, I'd better be off then," said Grandpa heading down the path. "If we're late for this train we won't make the connection."

"Bye, Grandpa," said Norm, closing the door and bounding up the stairs in double-quick time. There was a certain connection **he** had to make too. And there wasn't a moment to lose.

CHAPTER 21

Norm had scarcely clicked the mouse before a reply pinged back. He couldn't believe it. Not so much because it had happened so quickly, but because it had happened at all. He and his perfect cousin Becky were now officially friends. At least on Facebook they were, anyway. There was still more chance of Norm being abducted by aliens than there was of him and Becky ever being friends in real life.

Of course Norm had **_hoped_** Becky would confirm his friend request straightaway. He **_needed_** her to confirm straightaway if his cunning plan had the slightest chance of working. He hadn't really been **_expecting_** her to, though. He'd assumed she'd be way too busy doing something far more important and worthwhile than frittering away time on Facebook like **_normal_** human beings did.

Norm's plan – such as it was – involved posting something on his Facebook page which would somehow attract Becky's attention. But what? That was the problem. As far as Norm could see, the one and only thing that he and his cousin had in common **_was_** that they were cousins. Norm's mum and Becky's dad just happened to be brother and sister. That was all. Nothing else. Norm and Becky were merely twigs on the same branch of the same family tree.

A quick glance at Becky's own Facebook page soon confirmed what Norm already suspected: that it was scarcely possible Becky and Norm were from the same planet, let alone the same tree. Not only had she just been practising the piano, reading some stupid book and writing a poem about fluffy clouds, she was just about to bake "yummy-scrummy" courgette and cinnamon cupcakes. Yummy-scrummy? thought Norm. Pukey-flipping-wukey, more like.

And then Norm saw it. A message from one of Becky's friends saying she wasn't feeling very well and how she hoped she wasn't about to go down with some kind of bug. "Me too," Becky had replied. "Maths test tomorrow. Wouldn't want to miss that!"

OK, thought Norm. Two things. First of all, what kind of freak of nature **didn't** want to miss a flipping maths test? Actually didn't *want* to miss it? It was, quite simply, beyond Norm's comprehension. It didn't compute. He just didn't get it. Personally

Norm would have liked nothing more than to go down with some kind of stomach bug if it meant him missing a maths test. Second of all...

Norm stared at the screen. There **was** no second of all. That was it! *That* was how he was going to attract his perfect cousin's attention. By pretending he was ill! If Becky thought there was even the slightest possibility of catching something herself, she wouldn't want to come anywhere near the house tonight! Genius, thought Norm. Sheer flipping genius. Now all he needed to do was decide what was wrong with him.

It was then that Norm noticed the smell. A combination of rotten eggs and decomposing fish with a side order of overripe cheese, sprinkled with freshly grated socks.

"Phwoar!" said Norm, wrinkling his nose and wafting a hand in front of his face.

"Woof," said John from somewhere beneath the desk.

Norm was actually quite relieved. OK – so on the one hand he'd just inhaled a lungful of rancid cock-a-poo fart. On the other hand, at least he hadn't lost control of his bodily functions and let one go without realising it. And frankly, thought Norm, if he'd let one go quite *that* horrific, he wouldn't have to *pretend* he was ill at all. He really **would** be ill!

Wait a minute, thought Norm, his mind suddenly shifting up a couple of gears. He'd been licked full in the face by John only yesterday, hadn't he? And what had John been doing only seconds before that? Drinking from the flipping toilet, that's what! It wasn't just **possible** Norm had caught something – it was highly flipping **probable** Norm had caught something. It certainly sounded reasonable enough. It wasn't **too** far-fetched.

The question was, thought Norm, would Becky fall for it? Would it be enough to scare her off? Only one way to find out.

CHAPTER 22

Norm didn't know how long it would take for Becky to react. He didn't know for sure that Becky definitely **would** react. She was, after all, supposed to be busy making "yummy-scrummy" courgette and cinnamon cupcakes. She might not even see Norm's status update until it was too late. It really was just a question of waiting and seeing.

Rather than waiting and seeing by the computer though, Norm decided to ride his bike out on the street for a while.

"Hello, **Norman!**" said Chelsea from the other side of the fence, before Norm was halfway down the drive.

Gordon flipping Bennet, thought Norm. It was as if she'd been lying in wait for him. Like a...like a...like a...Norm couldn't think what it was like. Whatever it was like though, it was dead annoying and he wished she'd stop flipping doing it.

"What do **you** want?"

"Whoa!" said Chelsea. "Pardon me for breathing!"

"Is that it?" said Norm. "Can I go now?"

"Where to?"

"What?" said Norm.

"Where are **you** going?" said Chelsea. "Mikey's?"

"No," said Norm. "Why do you want to know?"

Chelsea smiled. "I think you **know** why I want to know, **Norman**."

Norm pulled a face. "Do I?"

"I think you **know** you do," said Chelsea.

Norm was getting confused. "You know that I know why you want to know?"

Chelsea smiled again. "You **know** I do."

"No I flipping don't!" said Norm, unable to contain his frustration any longer. "What are you on about? And don't even **think** about saying that I *know* – because I flipping **don't**, all right?"

"All right, **Norman**," said Chelsea. "Don't have a **baby!**"

"Well?" said Norm.

"What did he say?"

"Who? Mikey?"

"Yes, Mikey," said Chelsea.

"When?"

"This morning," said Chelsea. "Outside the supermarket. After I'd gone."

Finally! thought Norm. Why couldn't she just have said that in the first flipping place instead of going all round the houses?

"Did he tell you that I fancy him?"

"Erm…" said Norm.

"Erm what?" said Chelsea. "Did he, or not?"

Norm shrugged. "He might have mentioned it. Can't remember."

"He *might* have done?"

"OK, OK!" said Norm. "He told me that you fancy him."

Chelsea smiled. "And you actually *believed* him?"

"Uh? What?" said Norm. "Course I believed him!"

"*Yesss!*" said Chelsea, clenching a fist and punching the air.

Norm pulled a face. "You mean…"

"Are you serious?" laughed Chelsea. "Course I don't fancy him!"

"But..."

"I did it for a bet, **_Norman!_**"

Norm was gobsmacked. "A bet? Who with?"

"Chloe."

"Chloe O'Toole?" said Norm.

"Yeah, why?" said Chelsea. "What are you going to do about it?"

Good point, thought Norm. What **_was_** he going to do about it?

"Can I make a prediction?" said Chelsea.

Norm shrugged. "If you want."

"I don't think you'll do **anything** about it."

"Oh yeah?" said Norm.

"Yeah," said Chelsea.

"Well, we'll see about that then, won't we?" said Norm.

"Yeah, we will, won't we, **Norman?**"

The really annoying thing was, thought Norm, Chelsea was right. He probably **wouldn't** do anything about it. The really, **really** annoying thing was, Chelsea **knew** she was right. It was so un-flipping-fair.

"Can I have a word, love?" called Norm's mum from the front door.

"'Kay, Mum," mumbled Norm.

"Oh, hi, Chelsea!" said Norm's mum, spotting Chelsea on the other side of the fence.

"Hi!" said Chelsea with a cheery wave.

"How are you?" said Norm's mum.

"Very well, thank you," said Chelsea. "How are you?"

"Very well, thank you!" said Norm's mum.

Well, this is nice, thought Norm. Nothing like a cosy little chat the whole flipping street could hear.

"Norman?" said Norm's mum, with a tilt of her head.

"Coming, Mum," said Norm, turning his bike round and pedalling back up the drive.

"Run to mummy, there's a good boy," said Chelsea, loud enough for Norm to hear, but not his mum.

But Norm wasn't listening anyway. He was still reeling from the revelation that Chelsea had only ever **pretended** to fancy Mikey for a bet! How could anybody **do** that? Why would anybody **want** to do that? And to Mikey of all people. Mikey. His **best** friend, Mikey. Who wouldn't say boo to a flipping goose. And if he ever did he'd probably apologise to the flipping goose afterwards. It just wasn't right, thought Norm. It just wasn't on. It just wasn't flipping fair.

CHAPTER 23

Norm's mum was fishing around in her purse for change as Norm walked into the kitchen.

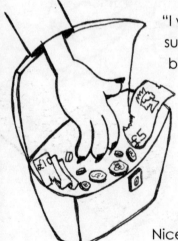

"I want you to pop to the supermarket and get some biscuits please, love."

Biscuits? thought Norm. Things were looking up all of a sudden.

"Nice ones," said Norm's mum.

Nice ones? thought Norm. So not the cheap own-brand ones they normally got then? How come? What was going on? Had they won the lottery or something? Did they even do the lottery? No one told Norm anything.

"What sort do you think she likes?"

"Who?" said Norm.

"Becky, of course!" said Norm's mum.

Of course, thought Norm. He might have flipping known. For a brief, delicious moment or two, he'd allowed his imagination to run riot and assumed that the biscuits might actually have been for him. Well, theoretically him and his brothers. But him, basically. Brian and Dave wouldn't have got anywhere near them.

"Nothing too fancy, I shouldn't think," said Norm's mum.

Nothing too flipping tasty either if Becky's preferred choice of cupcake was anything to go by, thought Norm. Was there such a thing as a courgette Hobnob?

"Just see what they've got, love," said Norm's mum, giving up looking for change and producing a ten-pound note instead.

"'Kay, Mum," said Norm, pocketing the money.

"Just remember they're for Becky – not you!"

"Course, Mum," said Norm setting off and coming face to face with his dad standing in the doorway.

"Funny you should mention that," said Norm's dad.

"Is it, Dad?" said Norm.

"Becky's not babysitting any more."

"Pardon?" said Norm, hardly daring to believe what he'd just heard.

"She just called to say she can't make it tonight."

"Oh dear," said Norm's mum. "That's a shame."

"Yesssss!!!" hissed Norm under his breath.

"What was that, Norman?" said Norm's dad, immediately suspicious.

"Erm, yes, that **is** a shame," said Norm. "But there's a lot of it about."

Norm's dad narrowed his eyes and fixed Norm with a look. "A lot of **what** about?"

Norm knew straightaway that he'd said too much. That he'd dug himself into a hole – and that it was time to try and climb out again. "Erm...whatever it is that Becky's got, Dad."

Norm's dad curled his lip. "Who said she's got anything?"

"Pardon?" said Norm, immediately realising that far from climbing **out** of the hole, he'd just managed to dig it even flipping deeper.

"Who said that Becky's actually **got** anything? All I said was that she couldn't make it tonight."

"Yeah, but I just presumed..."

"**Presumed?**" said Norm's dad.

"Well, I saw something on Facebook."

"Facebook?" said Norm's dad.

"Yeah," said Norm. "I think one of her friends has got a bug or something."

"You **think?**" said Norm's dad.

Gordon flipping Bennet, thought Norm. This must be what it felt like to be in court, being interrogated by one of those guys wearing a funny wig and a flipping Batman cape.

"Maybe she's being considerate and doesn't want **us** to catch anything!" said Norm's mum. "I wouldn't be surprised. She's such a nice girl."

Norm thought about this for a moment. It was true. Becky was such a flipping goody two-shoes that that was probably **exactly** what she was thinking! Maybe going to all that trouble becoming Facebook friends and posting something about a completely made-up dog-related disease hadn't been necessary at all. Shame really, thought Norm. Cock-a-poo flu was such a great name. As for one of the symptoms being a sudden urge to chase after sticks? Only one word for that. Sheer flipping genius.

"Go and get the biscuits anyway, love," said Norm's mum. "We'll think of something. Won't we, Alan?"

But Norm's dad didn't reply. The vein on the side of his head had begun to throb. Not that Norm noticed.

CHAPTER 24

For the second time that day Norm rode his bike through the woods to the supermarket. This time though, Norm locked his bike up outside like he was supposed to, instead of trying to take it into the store. It was just as well. Mr O'Toole was still on duty – and watching Norm like a hawk with a telescope.

Norm grabbed a basket and headed straight for the biscuits where he soon discovered there was a special promotion on Jammie Dodgers. And not just the supermarket's own-brand cheapo version either. **Proper** Jammie Dodgers.

The **real** deal. Buy one get one free.

Norm did a quick mental calculation. How many packets could he get for ten pounds? Mental calculations not being one of Norm's strong points however, Norm got his phone out and calculated it using that instead. He checked, double-checked and triple-checked. Each time he got the same answer. Thirty-two packets.

Thirty-two packets? thought Norm, beginning to load up his basket. Of Jammie flipping Dodgers? If ever there was an opportunity too good to miss, this was abso-flipping-lutely it.

"Oi!" said a voice.

Norm spun round to find Mr O'Toole glaring at him from the end of the aisle.

"What do you think you're doing?"

"BOGOF!" said Norm.

"What did you say to me?" said Mr O'Toole.

"BOGOF," said Norm. "Buy one get one free."

"Oh, right. I see," said Mr O'Toole. "So how many packets are you getting altogether?"

"Thirty-two," said Norm.

Mr O'Toole pulled a face. "Thirty-two?"

"Don't tell me," said Norm. "There's a rule, right?"

"What?" said Mr O'Toole.

"You're only allowed twenty-nine packets or less?"

"Are you being funny?" said Mr O'Toole.

"You tell me," said Norm, carrying on loading up his basket.

"What do you want thirty-two packets of Jammie Dodgers for anyway?"

Norm looked at Mr O'Toole. What did he *think* he wanted thirty-two packets of Jammie Dodgers for? Loft insulation?

"And you've got the money to pay for them?" said Mr O'Toole, without bothering to wait for Norm's reply.

"Yeah, course!" said Norm. "You don't think I was going to walk out without paying, do you?"

Mr O'Toole raised his eyebrows. "I didn't say that."

No, thought Norm. But he might as *well* have said it. It was outrageous, frankly. It was a whatsit. A slug on his character. Not a slug, thought Norm. A slur.

That's what it was. A slur on his character. Norm had half a mind to call his solicitor. The other half couldn't be bothered. And anyway Norm didn't actually **have** a solicitor. But that wasn't the point.

Norm sighed as he realised he'd lost count. How many packets of Jammie Dodgers was that?

"One, two, three, four, five..."

"Once I caught a fish alive."

grinned Mr O'Toole.

"Six, seven, eight, nine, ten..."

"Then I put it back again."

Norm took a deep breath. Mr O'Toole was obviously trying to wind him up – and so far, it had to be said, he was doing a pretty good job. When it came to being doughnuts of the highest order, thought Norm, Chloe and Ryan clearly took after their dad. Well, two could play at **that** game.

"How many's that now?"

"Enough," said Norm, starting to walk away.

"I'm watching you," said Mr O'Toole, following.

Excellent, thought Norm. That was the whole idea. There was something Norm needed to do. And he wouldn't want Mr O'Toole to miss it for all the flipping world. He wasn't absolutely sure that what he was about to do was against supermarket regulations. But even if it wasn't, it was bound to irritate Mr O'Toole. Which would be a very good thing indeed.

By now, Norm had reached his intended destination. There was only one can of Stynx left on the shelf after Mikey's shopping spree earlier on – but one can of Stynx was all that was required. Norm grabbed it, put  the basket down and whipped out his phone.

Taking a photo of himself was a skill that Norm had never quite been able to master. It didn't need to be a masterpiece though. As long as it was clearly Norm – and the Stynx was in shot – that was all that mattered as far as Norm was concerned.

Norm held the Stynx next to his face, stretched out his arm as far as it could go – and prepared to press.

"Cheeeeeeeeeese!" said Norm to himself.

"Oi! You can't do that!" said Mr O'Toole right on cue, just like Norm knew he would. Well, like Norm had **hoped** he would.

Norm took the photo. "Oops! Just did!"

"B-b-but…" Mr O'Toole spluttered.

Norm shrugged. "But what? What's the problem?"

Mr O'Toole didn't say anything. Mr O'Toole **couldn't** say anything. Mr O'Toole had gone purple. Mr O'Toole, as far as Norm could see, was **not** a happy bunny.

Mission accomplished, thought Norm. Well – the first part of the mission anyway. The second part would have to wait just a little bit longer to be accomplished. It no longer mattered that Dave had said he could handle things himself; Norm had changed his mind. Sometimes a big brother had to do what a big brother had to do.

CHAPTER 25

Norm snuck upstairs as soon as he got home. Within seconds he'd logged onto Facebook and finally accepted Ryan O'Toole as a friend. Facebook friend, that is. There was more chance  of Norm becoming an actual friend with his perfect cousin Becky than there was of becoming actual friends with Ryan O'Toole. And there was still more chance of discovering cheese on Mars than there was of Norm ever becoming actual friends with his perfect cousin Becky.

Hmm, thought Norm. Had Becky fallen for his cunning plan? Did she really think she'd catch cock-a-poo flu if she came to babysit? It didn't matter now anyhow. The main thing was that

Becky wasn't coming. This alone was cause for celebration. The fact that Norm had just managed to aggravate Mr O'Toole was the icing on the celebratory cake. Now all Norm had to do was post the photo of him holding the can of Stynx – and that would be the cherry on top of the icing on the celebratory cake.

A couple of clicks of the mouse was all that it took. A couple more clicks and Norm had tagged Ryan O'Toole in the photo, which meant that all Ryan's friends would get to see it. But would that be enough to get the message across? wondered Norm. Should he try and think of a caption to go with it to make it abso-flipping-lutely crystal clear to Ryan? Leave his little brother alone or else! But without actually saying that of course. Without making it too obvious? Without anyone being able to accuse Norm of doing to Ryan what Ryan had done to Dave!

"Don't even stink about it"? thought Norm. "One little squirt"? "Norm nose"?

Nope, thought Norm. Much too clever even if he did say it himself. After all it was a photo caption – not a flipping crossword clue!

As Norm stared at the screen, a message from Mikey suddenly pinged up.

thort of enything yet?

Whoa! thought Norm. How did Mikey know? He knew friends were supposed to be on the same wavelength – but this was ridiculous!

enything that rimes with chelsea i meen
said a second message, a moment or two later.

Oh right, thought Norm. So that's what Mikey was on about. He'd forgotten about that. The poem that Chelsea had written. And now Norm knew she'd written it for a flipping bet! Should he tell Mikey that Chelsea didn't really fancy him? Could he bring himself to actually do that to his best friend? No, thought Norm. He couldn't and he flipping well wouldn't. Some things were best left unsaid and that was definitely one of them. Besides, Mikey had been acting weirdly enough as it was lately what with all his hormones and stuff. That might well just tip him over the edge.

```
no sory
```
typed Norm.

Mikey's reply pinged back almost immediately.
dusent mater

Norm felt really bad. He wished he could have thought of a word that rhymed with Chelsea. Preferably a very rude one.

```
got lodes of jammy dogers tho
```
typed Norm, eager to change the subject.

bully 4u
fired back Mikey.

Bully for me? thought Norm. That was it! The caption for the photo! It was abso-flipping-lutely perfect! Anybody else seeing it might not understand. But Ryan O'Toole most certainly would!

"Bully 4 me" typed Norm, posting it with another click of the mouse.

Sorted, thought Norm. That was another thing crossed off the list. Not that Norm actually had a list, but it was satisfying all the same. The day was gradually getting better and better. And it wasn't very often Norm could say that.

"Norman?" yelled Norm's dad from the foot of the stairs. "Get down here at once!"

Oh well, thought Norm. It had been nice while it lasted.

CHAPTER 26

The Jammie Dodgers were piled up on the table when Norm walked into the kitchen.

"What do you call this?" said Norm's dad with a nod of his head.

"Dinner?" said Norm.

"Don't try and be smart with me, Norman. I'm not in the mood."

"When **will** you be in the mood?" muttered Norm.

"What was that?" said Norm's dad.

"Nothing, Dad," said Norm.

"I thought I said to get something **nice**, love," said Norm's mum, stepping in quickly before things got out of hand – which they were already threatening to do.

"You did, Mum."

"Well?"

Norm shrugged. "These **are** nice."

Norm's dad made the whoopee cushion sound with his lips. "You know perfectly well what your mother means, Norman! She told you to get something nice."

WHHOoooSHH!

Norm nodded. "I know."

"So why didn't you?"

"BOGOF," said Norm.

Norm's dad's expression instantly froze. It was if someone had hit the **_pause_** button.

"Buy one get one free," said Norm's mum, stepping in again.

"Oh, right," said Norm's dad, as if someone had hit **_play_** again.

"It was a bit selfish, don't you think, love?"

"Why?" said Norm. "I like Jammie Dodgers!"

"Exactly!" said Norm's dad. "**_You_** like them!"

Norm pulled a face. "I didn't think you'd mind."

Norm's mum and dad looked at each other for a second before turning back to Norm. Clearly they were awaiting some kind of explanation.

"Well, I mean, she's not coming any more, is she?" said Norm. "Becky?"

Norm's mum and dad glanced at each other again – then back to Norm again.

"What?" said Norm.

"You're going to have to pay for them," said Norm's dad.

Norm pulled another face. "I already **did**."

"I mean you're going to have to pay for them **yourself**, Norman."

"What?" said Norm.

"Oh, come on, Alan," said Norm's mum. "That's a bit..."

"A bit what?" said Norm's dad.

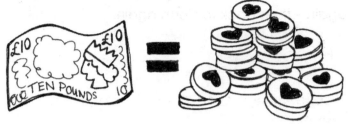

Unbe-flipping-lievable? thought Norm. They'd given him money to buy biscuits. He'd **bought** biscuits. Simple. End of.

"Do you think I'm stupid, Norman?"

Now possibly wasn't the best time to tell his dad what he really thought, thought Norm. "No, Dad. Course not."

"Do you think I don't know what's been going on?"

Norm wasn't altogether sure he knew himself – let alone whether his **dad** knew. And anyway, he was still stunned from the news that he was going to have to stump up for the Jammie Dodgers himself.

OK, so he'd got the tenner. The tenner his dad had given him for talking to Dave.

Less the bit he was going to give to Dave.

Less the bit he was going to give to Mikey for telling him the poem.

But that was hardly the point. There hardly was a flipping point. Why should **he** have to pay for the flipping biscuits? It wasn't **his** fault they were on special offer! What was he supposed to do? **Not** buy them, or something?

Norm's dad did the whoopee cushion thing again. "You're paying for them whether you like it or not."

Norm **didn't** like it. Since when did he have to actually **pay** for food? Next thing he knew they'd start charging him flipping rent! Well, it just wasn't on, thought Norm. The sooner he got a flipping solicitor the better.

"You left the computer on, Norman," said Norm's dad. "Again."

Gordon flipping Bennet, thought Norm. Not **another** lecture about switching stuff off and saving the flipping planet. If his dad spent less time banging on about that and actually did something himself for a change, the planet wouldn't **need** flipping saving!

"You were still logged into Facebook."

Oops, thought Norm. He hadn't reckoned on that happening. Now he knew what his dad had meant just now. His dad obviously knew **exactly** what had been going on.

"Cock-a-poo flu, Norman?"

Norm did his best to stifle a laugh. Despite the fact that he now knew his cunning plan had been rumbled, it was still funny to hear his dad actually say it.

"Was that really the best you could do?"

Please don't say it again, thought Norm.

"Cock-a-poo flu?" said Norm's dad.

That did it. This time Norm laughed out loud.

"Grow up, Norman," said Norm's dad, shaking his head.

"Sorry, Dad," said Norm, managing to stop himself laughing but unable to stop his shoulders shaking. And anyway, thought Norm, he wasn't sorry at all. He didn't particularly want to grow up. Well, he did – but in his own sweet time. He'd grow up when he **wanted** to. Not when he was flipping **told** to.

Norm's mum smiled. "Honestly, love. What are you like?"

It was a good question, thought Norm. What **was** he like?

"Top marks for ingenuity, I suppose," said Norm's dad.

Norm had no idea what **ingenuity** meant, but it sounded good. And there weren't too many things he got top marks for.

"Let's hope the new babysitter likes Jammie Dodgers!" laughed Norm's mum.

What? thought Norm. That was something else he hadn't reckoned on! He'd assumed his mum and dad wouldn't be going out any more. But it seemed he was wrong.

"New babysitter, Mum?"

"Of course!" said Norm's mum, breezily. "You didn't think we'd stay in just because Becky had cancelled, did you?"

"Course not, Mum," laughed Norm. "That would be ridiculous!"

The doorbell rang.

"That'll be her now," said Norm's dad.

"Her?" said Norm.

"Her," said Norm's dad, curling his lip like Elvis.

There was a sudden commotion from the hallway.

"I'll get it!" yelled Brian.

"No, I'll get it!" yelled Dave.

One of you flipping get it, thought Norm. He had a bad feeling about this. A **very** bad feeling. And as it happened – he was right to.

274

"Hello, Norman!"

said an all-too-familiar voice from the doorway.

Norm didn't have to turn round to know that it was Chelsea. So he didn't bother.

Norm's back...

THE WORLD OF NORM

MAY CAUSE IRRITATION

Jonathan Meres

Norm knew it was going to be one of those days when he woke up and found himself standing at a supermarket checkout, totally naked.

Jonathan Meres follows up the first Norm title, *May Contain Nuts*, with another laugh-out-loud story about Norm, a boy who can't understand why everything always seems unfair...

978 1 40831 304 6 £5.99 Pbk
978 1 40831 652 8 £4.99 eBook

ORCHARD BOOKS
Celebrating 25 Years
www.orchardbooks.co.uk

**Have you read the first hilarious NORM book?
Read on for the first chapter...**

CHAPTER 1

Norm knew it was going to be one of those days when he woke up and found himself about to pee in his dad's wardrobe.

"Whoa! Stop Norman!"
yelled Norm's dad, sitting bolt upright and switching on his bedside light.

"Uh? What?" mumbled Norm, his voice still thick with sleep.

"What do you think you're doing?"

"Having a pee?" said Norm, like this was the most stupid question in the entire history of stupid questions.

"Not in my wardrobe you're not!" said Norm's dad.

"That's from Ikea that is," added Norm's mum, like it was somehow OK to pee in a wardrobe that wasn't.

Norm was confused. The last thing he knew he'd been on the verge of becoming the youngest ever World Mountain Biking Champion, when he'd suddenly had to slam on his brakes to avoid hitting a tree. Now here he was having to slam on a completely different kind of brakes in order to avoid a completely different kind of accident. What was going on? And what were his parents doing sleeping in the bathroom anyway?

"Toilet's moved," said Norm, hopping from one foot to the other, something which at the age of three was considered socially acceptable, but which at the age of nearly thirteen, most definitely wasn't.

"What?" said Norm's dad.

"Toilet's moved," said Norm, a bit louder.

But Norm's dad had heard what Norm said. He just couldn't quite *believe* what Norm had said.

"No, Norman. It's not the *toilet* that's moved! It's *us* that's moved!"

"Forgot," said Norm.

Norm's dad looked at his eldest son. "Are you serious?"

"Yeah," said Norm, like this was the *second* most stupid question in the entire history of stupid questions.

"You *forgot* we moved house?"

"Yeah," said Norm.

"How can you *forget* we moved house?" said Norm's dad, increasingly incredulous.

"Just did," shrugged Norm, increasingly close to wetting himself.

"But we moved over three months ago, Norman!" said Norm's dad.

"Three months, two weeks and five days ago, to be precise," said Norm's mum, like she hadn't even had to think about it.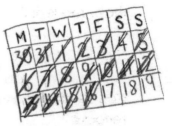

Norm's dad sighed wearily and looked at his watch. It was two o'clock in the morning.

"Look, Norman. You just can't go round peeing in other peoples' wardrobes and that's all there is to it!"

"I didn't," said Norm.

"No, but you were *about* to!"

Norm's dad was right. Norm *had* been about to pee in the wardrobe, but he'd managed to stop himself just in time.

Typical, thought Norm. Being blamed for something he hadn't actually done.

Norm considered arguing the point, but by now his bladder felt like it was the size of a space hopper. If he didn't pee soon he was going to explode. Then he'd *really* be in trouble!

"Go on. Clear off," said Norm's dad.

Norm didn't need telling twice and began waddling towards the door like a pregnant penguin.

"Oh, and Norman?"

"Yeah?" said Norm without bothering to stop.

"The toilet's at the end of the corridor. You can't miss it."

Norm didn't reply. He knew that if he didn't get to the toilet in the next ten seconds there was a very good chance that he *would* miss it!